Living with ADI

Read more by Zarin Virji

Gopal's Gully

Read more for middle-grade readers

Ninja Nani and the Bumbling Burglars by Lavanya Karthik
Ninja Nani and the Mad Mummy Mix-up by Lavanya Karthik
Ninja Nani and the Zapped Zombie Kids by Lavanya Karthik
Ninja Nani and the Freaky Food Festival by Lavanya Karthik
How to Win an Election by Menaka Raman
Against All Odds by Ramendra Kumar
Oops the Mighty Gurgle by RamG Vallath
The Deadly Royal Recipe by Ranjit Lal
Vanamala and the Cephalopod by Shalini Srinivasan
Flat-track Bullies by Balaji Venkataramanan
Pops by Balaji Venkataramanan
Ravana Refuses to Die by Rustom Dadachanji
Dhanak by Anushka Ravishankar and Nagesh Kukunoor
Simply Nanju by Zainab Sulaiman
Who's Afraid of a Giant Wheel by Zainab Sulaiman
Hot Chocolate Is Thicker than Blood by Rupa Gulab
The Sherlock Holmes Connection by Martin Widmark, Anushka Ravishankar, Katarina Genar and Bikram Ghosh
Tiger Boy by Mitali Perkins
Karma Fights a Monster by Evan Purcell
Karma Meets a Zombie by Evan Purcell
Karma vs the Evil Twin by Evan Purcell
The Hill School Girls: Alone by A. Coven
The Hill School Girls: Secrets by A. Coven
The Hill School Girls: Strangers by A. Coven
The Hill School Girls: Trouble by A. Coven
The Piano by Nandita Basu
Rain Must Fall by Nandita Basu
Starry Starry Night by Nandita Basu
Bim and the Town of Falling Fruit by Arjun Talwar
Vanamala and the Cephalopod by Shalini Srinivasan
When Blackbirds Fly by Hannah Lalhlanpuii
Ramanujan by Arundhati Venkatesh

Living with ADI

Zarin Virji

duckbill

An imprint of Penguin Random House

DUCKBILL BOOKS

Duckbill Books is an imprint of the Penguin Random House group of companies whose addresses can be found at global.penguinrandomhouse.com

Published by Penguin Random House India Pvt. Ltd
4th Floor, Capital Tower 1, MG Road,
Gurugram 122 002, Haryana, India

First published in Duckbill Books by
Penguin Random House India 2024

Copyright © Zarin Virji 2024

Zarin Virji asserts the moral right to be
identified as the author of this work.

All rights reserved

10 9 8 7 6 5 4 3 2 1

This is a work of fiction. Names, characters, places and incidents
are either the product of the author's imagination or are used
fictitiously and any resemblance to any actual person,
living or dead, events or locales is entirely coincidental.

ISBN 9780143466086

Typeset by Digiultrabooks Pvt. Ltd

This book is sold subject to the condition that it shall not, by way of trade
or otherwise, be lent, resold, hired out, or otherwise circulated without the
publisher's prior consent in any form of binding or cover other than that in
which it is published and without a similar condition including this condition
being imposed on the subsequent purchaser.

www.penguin.co.in

Adi Krishnan

I

I continue. To stare. At his shoes.

It's the strategy I was taught in Grade I.

Maintain eye contact when talking to people, except when you are being rebuked.

This instruction (font size sixteen, Arial Black) is printed on lime-green paper. The paper is pinned to the softboard above my study table.

Size ten brown brogues. Highly polished. Slightly scuffed. The shoes seem to merge with the dirty red carpeting that runs like an infection. All over the large room. From the desk in the centre to the mahogany bookcases on my left and, on the other side, to the steel cupboards on my right.

The same thing. Being repeated. Over and over again. In a nasal drone. As though a swarm of bees is let loose.

I can hear he is annoyed though I am not looking at him. If I look at someone, I find it difficult to follow what they are saying because I am so busy looking at them.

Kananbala stops abruptly. Has he ruptured a coronary artery? No, his health parameters appear to be stable.

'Hope you understand the gravity of the situation,' he says. Our eyes collide before I look down again with a slight nod.

His gaze shifts to the coordinator standing behind me at the doorway.

'Mrs Roberts, has the parent been called to take him home?'

'Yes, sir,' says Mrs Roberts.

'I would like to talk to the parent when she arrives.'

'Goes without saying, sir,' says Mrs Roberts, pushing me out of the principal's room.

In the lobby, forty-eight pairs of eyes look me up and down. My sick-as-hell classmates, the ones responsible for the mess that I am in. My class, IX B, is lined up against the floor-to-ceiling world map behind the glass case. I glare at them. No need to look down.

Mrs Roberts orders me to go to the classroom, pack my bag, come down and wait for Mom.

Familiar voices call out, 'Adi *manav*', and others join in with 'weirdo'. I walk past them without responding.

When I get back, the name-calling continues. Deftly, as usual, so that Mrs Roberts doesn't catch it at all. Her stern voice asks them to return to class and continue their studies. As if nothing has happened.

I stand near the main entrance with my belongings. When will Mom turn up? She must hear my side of the story before she meets Kananbala.

I pace up and down the lobby. Eighteen steps south. Eighteen steps north. Repeat.

'Adi? Adi Krishnan?'

The new housekeeping staffer is walking towards me. Her striped, blue uniform fits badly. They make one uniform size for all the housekeeping staff. This makes the fat ones look decidedly gross, and the thin ones' necks stick out of the shirts like vultures'. This one resembles a scavenging bird.

I nod.

'You left your water bottle in the class. *Aisa nahi karne ka*, what if one of your classmates had walked off with it? The cleaning staff would get blamed for no fault of ours.'

The bottle. Plonked in my hands. With a warning.

'Aditya, don't repeat this again.'

'My name's not Aditya. Just Adi!'

'Whatever.'

My name's a nuisance! Everyone thinks that Adi's short for Aditya. I have to explain that it's the short form of Ardeshir, the name of my maternal grandfather.

Then they make their second wrong assumption. That my lineage is Muslim. The name comes from Persia or Iran. I don't like explaining. That the name is common to Parsis and Shia Muslims, and Grandpa was Parsi.

Then people want to know the genesis of Krishnan.

Then I get bored and shout out, 'My dad's a Tamil Brahmin. My parents are divorced. I'm saddled with his name. Now please leave me alone!'

The choice of names is no better on the other side. It would be worse to be named Adi Daruwala. That's why Mom prefers to go with Delna D. Krishnan, although it's been ten years since her divorce.

Rarely do my classmates call me by my name. Mostly they say, 'Adi manav', 'weirdo', *'ghelo'*, *'gaando'* and other such assorted terms. This makes me laugh. What idiocy in the choice of terminology. Baseless. Illogical. Imprecise. How could I possibly be a prehistoric man? Neither does the dictionary definition of weird (strange, unusual or not natural) describe me accurately. Moreover, my grades clearly establish that I'm not 'ghelo' or 'gaando'.

I don't say all these things. When I speak, sometimes my voice comes out very loud. I don't know why. Maybe because I don't speak too much. Or maybe I don't speak too much because it can be loud. Everyone else around me seems to be able to control their voices without too much trouble. But I cannot.

When I want to launch my Weapons of Mass Destruction on my classmates, Mom stops me. 'You mustn't get violent, Adi. What if the point of the compass had pierced his eye? Learn to ignore these things. How many times must I spell out that they are jealous of your academic prowess?!' Yes, I agree that the 'eye for an eye' strategy makes the whole world blind. But Mom doesn't understand that I've got a right to defend myself.

Snakes don't bite unless they are hungry or threatened. It may appear that the common krait, India's most venomous snake, attacks a sleeping person without provocation. But that isn't true. The snake perceives the sleeping person's involuntary movement as dangerous.

'Stop walking about. Stand still; the paint may fall on you,' says the maintenance guy from up above. Perched on a ladder, he's touching up the board displaying the school motto, THINK-EXPLORE-ACHIEVE, placed high up on the wall above the entrance to the admin office.

I park myself on the visitors' bench. I loosen my tie. How much longer will I have to wait?

Shirin Ardeshir Daruwala

2

'And I forgot to tell you we'll be celebrating Christmas in Cape Town. It will be summer there, you know; it lies in the southern hemisphere. Cyrus has to make a business trip and he's going to take us along,' gushed my first-floor neighbour, Naju.

Now I understand why she called! Not to ask for the recipe for my strawberry tarts but to gloat about her more-than-perfect son-in-law who is forever whisking them off to exotic places.

'I feel bad, you know, an all-expenses paid vacation for me as well. I said to him, "You carry on with your wife and kids, why me?" But he never takes no for an answer. Bless him, he's so loving, Shirin. I don't know what I must have done to deserve such a good son-in-law. *Hiro chhe*. Every day I count my blessings.'

'Sorry, I've got a call waiting from Adi's school. Got to go, now. Bye!'

The call is a real lifesaver, but it couldn't be good news. My life is always about *pena maathi chula ma*.

Once again, Adi's in trouble. They tried calling his mother, but she didn't take the call, so it has to be Grandma who has to face the wrath of the principal.

A quick swipe at my wiry hair, my track suit will do, lipstick dabbed on, house keys, car keys sorted, I drive off to school. The afternoon traffic is bad but not too bad by Mumbai standards. In spite of the sky being overcast, the rain gods spare me, thank god. In twenty minutes, I make it to the school gate.

Where's that earth-shattering grind-groan-creak-clank coming from? Isn't the area around schools supposed to be a silent zone? Ah, I see it, the tenements next door have been pulled down and an excavator is throwing up stones and dirt. Now a fancy sixty-storeyed tower will come up with lavish living for the well-heeled. God knows where the tenement dwellers have been resettled. Mumbai is no longer a place for the middle or working classes.

Adi's stooped and lanky frame is visible even from a distance. The same dishevelled look as always, glasses fogged over. No other children around.

He rises as soon as he sees me enter the lobby.

'Why have you come? Where's Mom?'

'Is this the way to greet your grandmother, Adi? I drop everything; come racing here to bail you out and that's all you have to say!'

'Mamaiji, let me explain. It wasn't me—'

'Your stories can wait. Let me see the principal first, Adi.'

Waving him aside, I stride towards the office.

The admin assistant recognizes me at once; why wouldn't she? I'm one of the regulars. She leads me into the principal's office with a pitying look.

And I'm out in precisely ten minutes because, after years of practice, I know the drill. I have to hang my head low, agree with everything, end with, 'I'm so sorry, Dr Jose. I understand completely', bow my head further, fold my hands and get out.

This time it isn't even an act on my part; it is truly shocking. Adi has surpassed himself. It can't be called mischief, *dhoor ne dhefar*! The boy is an embarrassment to our family, that's all there is to it. And my darling daughter had better learn how to discipline him before it's too late.

'What did Kananbala say, Mamaiji? Am I really suspended for a whole week?'

'Of course, you are, Adi, and if I were the principal, I would not merely suspend you but jolly well expel you from the school for what you did. You should thank your stars you've got away lightly. And what did you just say? Kananbala?'

'All the students call him that. He's got hair coming out of his ears! Some students call him a bullfrog because of his bulging eyes. But I prefer Kananbala.'

Adi laughs like a hyena possessed.

'I will not have my grandson use these terms! Stop it, Adi! Let's go home now.'

'A week away isn't bad. It gives me time. To prepare. For my term exams.'

'And what about school fees going down the drain? As it is, for two lockdown years, your school enjoyed the fees for those so-called 'online lessons'—dhoor ne dhefar! It's July—barely two months into the new school year—and you will be missing school for a whole week.'

I walk down the steps, and he follows clumsily.

'Did you bring the car?'

'Yes, of course I did. Don't drag your feet, let's hurry home.'

'Are you mad at me, Mamaiji?'

He pulls my face towards him. Such a smart kid; now he'll pretend that he can't read facial cues. And my daughter, his greatest ally, will support him fully.

'Adi, I'm not getting into a discussion now about what you did. Move it; I want to drop you home before the traffic goes crazy.'

Pushing his hands away, I hold him by the elbow and lead him towards the car and into the back seat. I hate him sitting in the front beside me, his fingers fidgeting with the controls panel; it makes me nervous.

'Don't you want to see the still life that I painted in the art period, Mamaiji?'

'I certainly don't. Just sit still while I take you home.'

The phone begins to ring just then. Has to be Delna. I'm in no mood to enter into a lengthy conversation.

'Yes, we are coming home. No, I won't tell you what happened on the phone. Wait till I get home. What? Adi, he's absolutely fine; what could be wrong with him?'

Adi leans over to snatch the phone from my hands, but I hold on to it and fling it into my bag as soon as my conversation ends.

Thankfully, he keeps quiet until we turn into the lane to their building.

'Can we pick up a packet of chips, Mamaiji? My favourite—the cheese and onion ones. Please give me twenty rupees.'

Remorse is not his middle name, dhoor ne dhefar!

'Do you think we are on a picnic, Adi?'

'No, we are returning home from school, Mamaiji.'

'Exactly. We are not stopping for anything, Adi.'

'Okay.'

Parking is nearly impossible in their pocket-sized compound and now more so with on-going repairs.

I drop him at the gate, back up and squeeze myself between two SUVs in the lane. Maruti Alto, zindabad!

The lift is out of order, so here I am climbing up four floors. One of these days, my arthritic knees will give up on me; mark my words. A million times I must have told Delna to move in with me, but her answer is always, 'No, Mummy, I must be independent.' And so, she continues to live in that crummy two-bedroom apartment in MIG Colony, Bandra East, regardless of my exhortations.

Shirin Ardeshir Daruwala

3

By the time I make it up, the door to their flat is ajar, and the reception committee is ready to pounce on me.

'Mamaiji, please sit. Lemme get you a glass of water.'

That's Jasmine, my girl! She takes the bag out of my hands and ushers me to the sofa. 'Sofa' is too grand a word for that wretched piece of furniture. Cane sofas are the pits, but Delna can't afford anything better. I adjust myself the best I can on its sagging *gaddi*, but in no time, its ribs begin to poke at my backside.

'I'll get the water, Jas. And let me put the kettle on for Mamaiji's tea,' says Suryamani, bounding into the kitchen.

Delna is fussing over Adi in the corner as though a victorious boxer has returned from the ring. She couldn't hug and kiss him of course, because he's such a touch-me-not.

She advances towards me with accusations in her eyes. She's in her usual drab one-size-too-big dull grey khadi kurta, tall and thin as a flattened Bombay duck, runny kohl in her eyes and unkempt hair.

'My son is not saying a word. He's cold and clammy. He's traumatised. Please tell me what happened, Mummy,' she says, crossing her hands and sitting across from me, her voice terse. Adi sits next to her.

'I'll tell you what happened. Adi yanked Dr Jose's hair to find out if it was real or a wig.'

Jasmine's eyes widen. 'Seriously? And was it a wig, Adi? That must have been so embarrassing for Kananbala,' she says, ruffling her brother's hair. She was the only one allowed to touch him.

Suryamani hands me the glass of water and asks Jas to translate what was said into Hindi as she doesn't understand English well. Jas does, and both of them titter.

'It wasn't a wig. But hear how it started,' says Adi.

Jas and Suryamani sit cross-legged on the floor, looking at Adi expectantly.

'I'm all ears,' says Jas, cradling her ear in the palm of her hand and leaning towards him.

'That's punny. All about ears!' says Adi.

'OMG, Adi. I'm dead,' goes Jasmine.

Both the brother and sister cackle.

'Your children think it's some kind of joke! I better get going.' I try to raise myself from that godawful sofa.

'Sit, Mummy, let's listen to Adi for the full story,' says Delna, her voice on edge. 'I don't like what I'm hearing, Adi, so you'd better tell us everything.'

'Last week's test results were declared. I got twenty out of twenty,' says Adi.

'My baby brother, always first! But you told me you had made a calculation error, Adi, didn't you?' Jasmine gets up, pats his head and gets back to the floor in one fluid movement. *Mari nalli, mari mitthi*, she could well be a ballerina!

'No, everything was perfect! Mohit and Riya were mad because they got sixteen out of twenty. At break, everyone went out. I could hear them playing "Truth or Dare". I was solving the next exercise. Someone said Kananbala was on his rounds, so they trooped in.

Mohit came up to me saying, "Okay, wise guy, we don't have much time. We dare you to pull Kananbala's hair. There's a strong rumour that he wears a wig."'

'You could have refused, Adi.'

'They had formed a circle around my desk and … I guess I was scared. Like there's no escape. I didn't know how I would reach Kananbala's head. But he bent down to pick up a piece of paper. I went up behind him and seized his hair. But it wasn't coming off. I applied greater force, but nothing happened. Kananbala straightened, and charged at me like a rabid hippo, screaming, "What are you trying to do, Adi Krishnan?"

'I told him that it was part of the game, but he rushed off. We were all summoned downstairs. I was the only one called inside where he gave me a lecture for thirty minutes.'

'Your classmates are rascals, Adi,' says Delna. 'I will take this up with Mrs Roberts.'

'His classmates may be rascals, but what about Adi? Surely this highly intelligent fourteen-year-old can understand that he can't get away with such a prank!'

'Mummy, you know how Adi is. The class provoked him to do this stupid thing, and they've gone scot-free, and my poor son is suspended!'

'Delna, are you trying to say your son is blameless? Dhoor ne dhefar! Don't even start on that spiel about your son and his condition. You know I don't agree with your opinion. It's plain and simple bad behaviour; mark my words.'

Delna and I stare at each other, our eyes blazing.

'The water must have boiled by now. Let me get the tea!'

Suryamani's sprung up to save the situation. She's not only efficient, but she's also got the pulse of this family right.

'Come to the dining table, everyone, for tea and bhakra. Mamaiji, your bhakras were so good, there's hardly any left now,' says Jasmine, collecting my glass with one hand and rescuing me from that miserable sofa with her other hand.

'I don't want anything. I'm going in.' Adi stomps into his bedroom, slamming the door behind him.

'Now he'll go and sit in the bathroom for hours, Mom,' says Jasmine.

'Let him stew for a while, Jas. It's okay,' says Delna, not siding with her son for a change.

Suryamani learnt how to make mint-and-lemongrass tea from me, and mark my words, now she makes it better than I can. Everyone's quietly munching on my bhakras.

'Mamaiji, I want to learn how to make bhakras from you! Honestly, they are the *bestest* I've ever eaten! Even Sid loved them.'

'That explains why there are so few left,' chuckles Delna. 'Suryamani, why didn't you inform me about the vanishing bhakras?'

'Mom, I did tell you, remember?'

'Sweetie, I'm just joking. Of course, you can take them for Sid or any of your friends.'

Nice boy, that Sidney—Catholic family, parents are doctors, duplex apartment at Marine Drive, a huge property in Goa. I would be overjoyed if Jas and Sid were to get serious.

Whenever I suggest this to Delna, she begins to rant. 'Mummy, they are just seventeen. Isn't it too early to think of anything long-term? My getting married at twenty-two was a huge mistake, wasn't it? My PhD was abandoned to love's bloom, the marriage disintegrated and what am I left with now, except bills to pay each month?'

That was true, of course. Delna rushed into marrying Krish, the children followed. And she could never get back to her studies in political science. Never mind that. I'm going to encourage Jas to pursue Sid. No harm.

'Nothing much to bhakras, Jas. All you need is good toddy. The sap must be extracted early morning and left aside to ferment for less than two hours. I'll make a fresh batch for Sid's family whenever you like. What say?'

'Mamaiji, you are the best. Both Sid and I can come over to help you!'

'That would be lovely, Jas! *Chalo*, I had better get going, or else this peak hour traffic will get me.'

'Thanks for going to Adi's school today, Mummy. My department was hosting an event; I couldn't leave, you know how it is,' says Delna, her face drawn.

'You know you can depend on me, Delna. How did the event go?'

'Very well. We had two scholars from Harvard talking about the current situation in Kashmir.'

'That must have been interesting.'

'When are you gonna come again, Mamaiji?'

'Let's see, sometime next week.'

I can't help squeezing Jas's cheeks.

'That's too far away!'

Crushing me in her embrace and smothering me with kisses, she rocks me. It helps that we are both the same height.

'*Baba re baba*, you all are forgetting something,' says Suryamani. 'We have guests for dinner on Saturday!'

'Oh shoot!' says Delna. 'How could I forget? Krish and family must have arrived from Singapore today! You promised you'd be here with us, Mummy!'

'That was the 30th, wasn't it?' My eyes seek confirmation from Jasmine.

'Man, that's the day after!' says Jas.

'Fine, I'll be here. Do you want me to make anything other than caramel custard?'

'No, Suryamani and I will take care of the rest,' says Delna. 'But Mummy, please don't tell Krish about Adi's suspension.' Her tone softens; she's folding her hands to me, my high-and-mighty daughter.

'Why not? As Adi's father, he has every right to know what's going on in his life!'

'Mummy, you know how Krish is. He'll start that thing about changing schools again, and I don't want any more stress. Besides, we are meeting his wife and son for the first time so let's just be nice to each other and have a pleasant evening.'

She bends down to kiss me, that's how desperate she is.

'Fine, as you say. But you better watch out. Adi may be the first one to blurt it out, mark my words.'

'I'll handle Adi, don't worry.'

Her words don't reassure me at all.

Jas and Suryamani escort me down to the car.

Adi Krishnan

4

Suspension week. Not bad at all. Invigorating, in fact.

The homework for the week is done on the first day. Revision remains to be done. Also the physics project. What's more important is that I can paint, read, talk to the crows and do whatever I fancy.

Mom left strict instructions to make nothing but dal-chawal as a punishment for my suspension. But Suryamani made my favourite eggplant parmesan with French fries. Even though Jas is dieting, she eats heartily. 'For the cause,' she says. The pact among the three of us was that we would finish every last crumb. So that Mom wouldn't come to know what was cooked.

Jas is home early. She can't stand the physics prof. Now she's in Mom's room, on the phone with Sid. This will go on for a couple of hours. Although they were together all morning.

I've asked her several times if they are boyfriend-girlfriend. She shrugs her shoulders and gives me *gyan*. Her face reddens and her dimples deepen.

'He's a boy, he's my bestest friend, and that's what matters.'

'Is he or isn't he your boyfriend?'

'Call him boyfriend or not. You like him, don't you, Adi?'

Yeah, he's decent. Never bothersome.

I have read all about the infatuation syndrome—yuck. She was a slave to her hormones. Mine are totally under my command. Mom says, wait a year or two. I say I'm not going to fall for these cheap tricks that love plays.

Mom calls to check on me. She instructs me to help Suryamani with the dusting and polishing of the brassware. Why me? She says it's suspension protocol. She can't be serious. She gets me to do these chores every weekend, too.

The house is being spruced up for Dad's visit, so there's one or two extra things. I didn't mind Dad's coming; I haven't seen him since the lockdown. But to bring along the new wife and a squealing infant! That was totally unnecessary. Why did he want to inflict his new family upon us? If only I could slither away unnoticed like a smooth snake to escape this encounter with Dad's second family.

Smooth snakes inhabit the shrubby meadows of southern England. Very little is known about them because they are rarely seen or heard.

Mom and Jas think it's pretty cool. They can't wait to meet the new family. I don't like new people.

Mamaiji calls and speaks to Suryamani and Jasmine. I'm persona non grata for her.

Jas tries to talk Mamaiji into pleading her case with Mom. This time, the subject is tattoos. Mamaiji promises to talk to Mom. I don't know Mom's views. I can't understand why anyone would get themselves tattooed. I don't even like people touching me.

As soon as her conversation with Mamaiji ends, I speak up. 'Jas, why do you want a tattoo?'

'MYOB, Adi. I like tattoos, that's why.'

'Jas, getting inked. It's painful. Sheer torture.'

'Most times I don't mind your staccato speech, Adi, but right now it's infuriating, so please spare me. And BTW, haven't you heard the proverb, "no pain, no gain", Adi?'

'It can cause an allergic reaction or skin infections. And if the equipment is not sterilized, you may even contract a bloodborne disease.'

'Thanks, *Dr Adi Krishnan*, for your advice! FYI, many of my friends have tattoos, and no one's dead yet. And don't you dare tell Mom about it before I get a chance to speak to her!'

'Okay, suit yourself.'

I go down for a few rounds on my bicycle. To build muscles. To gain height. One way to rid myself of the labels 'scarecrow' and 'aneomo'. I like being outside. It is calming, even in the middle of the crowded city.

When I get back, Jas is on the phone with Vibha, her bestie. Her back is to me, but I can hear her part of the conversation.

'You know the gulmohar tree behind the canteen? Sid and I were sitting under it this morning. The sunlight peeking through those leaves and a cool breeze blowing—that sort of atmosphere. I could have fallen asleep, but Sid kept poking me to remind me of the bell for the maths class. Those leaves, Vibs, are so feathery or frilly, I don't have the words to describe them—'

'Gulmohar leaves are like coriander.'

'Chhee, Adi! You know I hate coriander; you are such a spoiler!'

'Fern-like. Compound leaves. Doubly pinnate.'

'Keep your gyan to yourself, Adi. Anyway, why are you sneaking up on me and listening to my conversation?'

She turns to face me, her eyes blazing.

'You were looking for the right word, weren't you?'

'Thanks, Adi. I can manage.'

She pushes me out of the room, and the door is slammed in my face. So much. For being kind. To my big sis!

Better get cleaning with Suryamani. Earn some brownie points before Mom's arrival.

Shirin Ardeshir Daruwala

5

Seems like we are set for a good evening with my daughter's ex-husband and his new family.

The lift's working, the tiny living room seems to have expanded and the godawful sofa's got a firmer gaddi. Of course, Delna didn't buy it—how could she? She's always broke; she borrowed it from Harish, her next-door neighbour, along with the leopard print cushions.

The berry pulao's turned out well except that it's slightly burnt at the bottom of the pan. The *papeta-par-eeda* could have done with a little less salt but will do. The paneer kofta curry and the chicken chettinad have come from her neighbourhood restaurant. I knew very well that Delna wouldn't manage to rustle up any more dishes but she's too proud to ask for my help.

Adi's glasses are not fogged up for a change, and he's being helpful, assisting Jas to lay the table.

Suryamani is cutting up onions and cucumber for a salad. Delna's wondering, a little too late, whether she should have ordered red wine for the evening, or the mixed fruit juice will do.

As for me, I enjoy a glass of wine now and then but it's in Delna's best interest not to go overboard entertaining Krish and family. Krish should realize how hard it is to run a household on one salary and the pittance that she receives as alimony does not allow her to wine and dine her guests whenever she wants.

The chime of the doorbell sends Delna running to the door. It's only the *pavwala* so everyone goes back to what they are doing except Suryamani, who collects the bread and eggs for the next day.

Delna sits next to me; she's not looking bad at all—red is her colour. The red-and-white freshly ironed Madhubani-print kurta with white palazzo pants make her look less skinny, the lip gloss and kajal accentuate her best features and her wispy hair is gathered into a loose bun. Why can't she dress like this more often?

Once more, the bell goes and Jasmine sprints to the door. It's the neighbours, the guys they call H&M—Harish and Mandar—grinning widely, a box of *mithai* in Harish's hands.

'Hello everyone! Can you believe it? We've completed one year as your neighbours! Just wanted to share some sweets—with thanks from H&M for all your help,' says Harish, handing the box to Delna.

'By the way, can we borrow some yoghurt? We are having unexpected guests and need to whip up a raita real quick.' That's Mandar, the smooth talker.

I think half of Delna's groceries end up in their bellies. She goes on about them being a pair of young bachelors in need of a helping hand, but I don't get it. They are both highly paid guys in the ad world. They could easily employ a domestic helper who can shop, cook and clean for them. Some hanky-panky happening, mark my words. They are probably in a relationship, and they don't want anyone coming or going; in short, no tongues wagging.

Who am I to say anything more? My own son Ruzbeh, in faraway New York, thirty-eight years old, never married. He has been living with his flatmate Nathan for eight years now. A mother's instinct says that there is more than the *just friends* nonsense that he tells me.

Jas and Delna are hugging H&M and congratulating them. For what, I wonder.

Seconds after their exit, Krish and family arrive. The baby in Krish's arms is squirming and bawling to high heaven, with Geetha smiling by his side.

As Delna rises to greet them, Krish says in his booming voice, 'I'm so sorry, Venky's uncomfortable because his pamper's soiled. Can Geetha get him changed first, and then we can settle down for a good evening?'

Krish hands the baby to Geetha as she releases one of her bags into his hands.

'Yes, of course,' says Delna, leading her into the bedroom. Geetha says 'Hi' to everyone and races in with Venky.

Krish is looking happier and more prosperous with a growing belly and a receding hairline. As VP of a Singaporean bank loans division, he must be making a pile.

'My children, how are you doing?' He hugs them both. Jas returns his hugs whole heartedly with kisses thrown in as well. Adi stands stiffly.

Krish comes over to me. 'Mrs Daruwala, how nice to see you! You look just the same, evergreen. Can't wait to taste your heavenly cooking, I say.'

He's always been respectful and affectionate towards me. Never quite understood why their marriage fell apart—Delna's fault mostly, I suppose. Mark my words, Krish mustn't have given in to her pugnacious ways. They could never see eye-to-eye about bringing up Adi. Adi's delayed milestones and childhood tantrums were enough to send Delna scurrying to this doctor and that, getting one test done and then another until she was convinced about his ASD or neurodivergence or whatever fancy term the doctors offered.

I tried my best to assure her based on my own experience that boys develop slower than girls. But my daughter was adamant. Dhoor ne dhefar, half the Parsi population would be termed neurodivergent if we went looking for minute eccentricities. And then she started wasting money on occupational therapy and what-not, all the time treating Adi with kid gloves, instead of disciplining him the old-fashioned way. Her obsessive care for Adi must have created the wedge between them, mark my words.

Now there's really no point looking back, Krish has certainly moved on, and I don't blame him one bit. My own daughter never knows what's good for her; mark my words.

'Mamaiji's made caramel custard for you, Dad, your favourite!' gushes Jas, coming up to Krish and encircling her arms around his midriff.

'Is it still your favourite, Dad?' asks Adi.

'Yes, Adi, of course. If you ask the doctors, I shouldn't be having any sweets. But tonight is an exception, of course.' Krish winks at Adi. 'Adi, you've really shot up since I saw you last! You must be 5'8" or something like that. Are you the tallest boy in the class, my son?'

'No. That's Mohit. Almost six feet tall.'

'What about me, Dad?' goes Jas, looking up at Krish, eyes dancing with devotion.

She really misses having a father figure. Monthly Zoom calls, dhoor ne dhefar, can't compensate for a proper father-daughter relationship. What she really needs in her teenage years is a solid male presence. If only Delna would consider remarriage, but then again, who would want to marry a barely-making-ends-meet college lecturer with two kids? Difficult, to say the least.

'You are growing more beautiful by the day, my fragrant flower, my *sakkarakutti*, now a college goer and all!' Kissing her forehead, Krish wraps his arms around her.

Jasmine glows.

'You haven't answered her question, Dad. She's asking if she's grown taller. She's barely grown an inch since you saw her last,' says Adi. That boy can't hold his tongue, never.

'No cap, I'm 5'2" now, same as Mamaiji!'

She runs over to punch him, Adi dodges, retreats and almost steps on Venky, who's taking unsteady steps out of the bedroom followed by the two women. Venky screams, and both the women bend down to see if he's fine.

'Come to Daddy, Venky!' Krish rushes forward and picks him up. 'Let's give him some time to get used to everyone. He's a friendly little fellow, actually.'

'Hello again,' Geetha smiles at all of us. 'I feel as if I already know everyone! Krish, you haven't given the gifts yet!'

'Oh, my bad. Here, Adi, the books you wanted—about venomous snakes. And hope you like this pair of sneakers, Jas. Some chocolates for everyone.'

Both the children thank him and take the gifts into their room. When they return, Delna says, 'And what about our gift for Venky?'

'What was the need for this?' says Geetha, politely and prettily.

'It's our custom. C'mon, Jas, let's do a little Parsi-style ceremony to welcome Venky!' Delna motions her towards the kitchen.

'We call it *achhu-michhu*—it's done for birthdays, weddings, everything auspicious,' says Jasmine, rushing into the kitchen.

She fetches the low stool with the chalk-patterned rangoli. Venky is made to sit on it. He's garlanded and blessed with a red dot on his forehead and showered with rice grains. The gift-envelope and coconut are handed to Geetha. Thankfully, Venky sits quietly through the whole exchange, only reaching for the envelope when it's all over.

I can't help saying, 'Already interested in money, like his father!'

Everybody grins.

Geetha says, 'You are so right, Mrs Daruwala. Let me do a *namaskara* on behalf of Venky.'

She tries to touch Delna's feet, but Delna stops her and hugs her instead. Krish looks relieved to see the two women sharing good vibes.

Geetha's quite dishy-looking; must be a change from Delna, I imagine. And so well turned out, shoulder-length hair and make-up perfectly done. She and Krish, twinning in black designer wear, make a great-looking couple.

Delna scoots off to the kitchen and scoots back with a tray of drinks and chips.

Krish regales us with his exploits at the bank; lockdown stories are exchanged, as expected. By now, Venky's started exploring the room but refuses to give in to Jasmine's advances. I must say I thought the evening would be awkward, but it's swimming along pretty well. It's especially good to see Delna and Geetha agreeing with each other on everything possible. This is what modern families are all about; mark my words.

The meal is appreciated by our guests, and we settle down for dessert. After complimenting me on the lightness of the custard, Krishnan turns to Adi. 'How is school going, *kanna*? Top of the class, I hope?'

Adi responds, 'Do you mean in the present tense or the past tense?'

Delna cuts in nervously, 'In general, Adi. That's what Dad means.'

'Yes, of course, generally. How has your week been?' prompts Krish.

'Scored twenty out of twenty on my maths test but the week . . . it was cut short for me. I've been at home for two days. I was suspended . . . for no fault of mine.'

There, I knew it would come out of Adi's mouth sooner or later!

'Suspended? How dreadful, I say! What happened?' goes the dad, dripping with concern when he's hardly had any hand in Adi's upbringing.

Delna narrates the whole story, taking care to paint her son in as good a light as possible, yet the mood in the room darkens.

'If you ask me, this school stinks, Delna. Just as I thought. State board schools are stuck in a rut. They haven't moved with the times. We need to seriously consider a better environment for him,' says Krish.

'Shall we drop this topic for now? We can discuss it another day, just you and me, Krish.'

Delna, my pit bull of a daughter, sounds very soft and subdued for a change.

'How about some coffee for everyone?' Delna's conciliatory tone doesn't fool anyone.

'Yes, we can take it up later, but don't you think it's becoming more urgent now? Adi, my son, you deserve a world-class school.'

'I'm not going to change the school. That's final!' says Adi. He flings his dessert bowl to the floor and storms out of the room.

Everyone's silenced. Delna bends down to pick up the pieces. Krish clears his throat and turns to Jasmine.

'That was quite an outburst from your brother, Jas!'

'Krish, how many times have I told you that Adi's different? He's high-strung! Even his doctor thinks—' Pit-bull Delna is back in form as she gets up.

'Don't bring his doctor into this, Delna. You know I don't agree with you about his so-called diagnosis. He's quite normal, if you ask me. Look at his grades.'

'He's like any teenager, I suppose,' smiles Geetha, making an effort to lighten the atmosphere.

'Not exactly, Geetha. I don't want to discuss this any further right now, if you please,' says Delna through clenched teeth.

Conveniently, Venky starts bawling again, and Geetha signals that they should be leaving.

Apologizing for Adi's behaviour, Delna keeps repeating, 'He's a sensitive child.'

Geetha nods understandingly, but the damage is done. A perfectly pleasant evening gone kaput.

Delna D. Krishnan

6

What an interminable wait at the clinic, and it's not even a Saturday. And yet, I'm glad about this interlude, if I could call it that. Because there are few moments like these when I have time to collect my thoughts or to just sit back and do nothing.

Thank goodness I could switch lectures with Sujata and take half a day off. She's a real buddy; understands me like very few people do.

Thankfully, Adi's got his nose in the snake book so he'll be fine. I wish Mummy were here to see how many children have ASD or mental health issues. She never misses an opportunity to rub it in that Adi behaves atrociously, without any consideration for the underlying causes. At other times, she thinks it's my skills as a mother that are responsible for how Adi behaves, forgetting conveniently how Jasmine's turned out.

Eventually, we are summoned into Dr Parekh's office. The doctor's her usual self, not a hair out of place, starched cotton sari, pearls and the big red bindi on her forehead, calm and business-like.

She has been my main source of calm and support all these years. From helping me work on his speech to explaining the importance for schedules, assisting me to appreciate Adi's need for space and that his social awkwardness does not mean that he hates people— she has shown me so many ways to be a better mother to him and let him be himself and independent.

'How are you today, Adi?' asks Dr Parekh.

'I'm fine. How are you?' says my son and heir in his robotic voice, with a half-smile. He glances in my direction for approval.

'What's new, Adi? I'm sure you are going to quiz me about something or the other,' says Dr Parekh, running her practised eye over Adi.

'Do you know which is the longest venomous snake in the world, Dr Parekh?'

'Hmmn . . . is it the king cobra?'

'Correct. And the second longest?'

'I don't think I know. You tell me, Adi?'

'The black mamba. Found in sub-Saharan Africa. Grows to a length of 2 to 3 m.'

'Really? Didn't even know about the existence of a snake called black mamba! My GK grows by leaps and bounds in your company!'

Adi takes the sketch of the black mamba from my bag and offers it to her for her display board, which is filled with children's work.

'What an accomplished artist you are! Thank you, Adi,' says the doctor. 'This sketch will definitely go up on my wall, as usual.'

Excitedly, Adi continues, 'Look at his mouth! It's coffin-shaped. When you look at him, it's like staring into the eyes of death!'

'Adi, thanks for educating me as always about a new topic, but I'm afraid we'll have to cut short this conversation. You must have seen the number of children waiting outside,' says the doctor, turning to me.

Adi sits back, disappointed.

I tell the doctor all that happened at school. She listens intently with her head cocked to one side, typing notes on her desktop. When I'm done, she turns her attention to Adi and starts deconstructing the event leading up to his suspension. Adi says 'yes' and 'no'; I'm not even sure if he's listening to her or simply waiting for this discussion to be over and done with.

Then she asks me to leave. Adi looks at me as if he wishes he could follow. I'm out of the door before he can open his mouth.

I don't know if these sessions do any good these days, but at least I'm doing something rather than twiddling my thumbs. Most of the time, I feel as lost as anyone else in understanding Adi's condition, but I can't say this to Krish or Mummy; I have to put up a front that I've got everything under control. From the very beginning, Krish has ~~been dismissive of~~ never really acknowledged Adi's disorder; I guess he just can't accept that his son is anything short of perfect. Thank goodness for Dr Parekh and for the ASD support group; it's the only space where my anxieties can be openly expressed without fear of being judged.

Adi's come a long way from the three-year-old who would stand in a corner and rock front to back, with a steady hum, without any eye contact. Occupational therapy sessions, coupled with determined efforts from Jasmine and myself, have helped to bring Adi to this level. Now he's functioning like so-called normal children of his age, except for certain markers: his love for set routines and his dislike of change, his inability to understand figurative language and his general social awkwardness. Despite being on the autism spectrum, Adi's got away lightly. I've seen other children with ASD who face far worse challenges lifelong, and the uphill task faced by their parents is unimaginable to me.

Ten minutes later, Adi's out, and the doctor calls me in.

'Let's increase his dosage of the night drug, Delna,' she says.

'But doctor, he's barely able to wake up on time for school with the current dosage.'

'The school can surely exempt him from attending the first period if I give a letter?'

'The school is quite strict . . . It's a traditional school, doctor. They believe in following the rules rigidly, to say the least.'

'I see. Alternatively, can he go to bed earlier so that he gets a minimum of ten hours of sleep?'

'Rather difficult because he likes to read and paint before going to bed. I'll have to enforce that, I guess.'

'You'll have to. Or talk to the school. They may not be as unreasonable as you expect.'

'Oh shoot, almost forgot! I wanted to get your thoughts on something, about a change of schools, doctor. My ex-husband is keen that Adi shifts to a more progressive school—a school with an ICSE or an international curriculum—that handles children more sensitively. Do you think it's a good idea?'

She smiles. 'We all went to state board schools, didn't we, Delna, and turned out quite all right?! But it's a trend sweeping through India at present; perhaps these schools are better, who knows? In fact, Adi brought it up in our conversation more than once; he's terrified about going to a new school. Not advisable, in my opinion. Children like Adi don't adapt well to change.'

'Exactly what I was thinking, doctor. I'm so glad you agree! Anything else, Dr Parekh?'

'I think we are done. Take an appointment for next month, and you take care of yourself, Delna. You are looking quite stressed yourself.'

Dr Parekh dismisses me with a short wave of her manicured hand. God knows when I had a manicure last. No time or money for these ~~indulgences~~ niceties. Like hell, I can pamper myself, on top of everything else.

'Wasn't I well-behaved, Mom? What did the doctor say? Did she complain about me?'

Adi's tugging at my handbag, not even waiting till I finish paying the doctor's assistant.

'Complain? Of course not, Adi. Let's talk when we get home.'

₹1,200 for a thirty-minute session, and the doc must be seeing ten to twelve patients a day. Really nice, she's making big bucks while my life . . . ! She can sit in her air-conditioned office and offer a listening ear, filling out a prescription now and then. She doesn't have to take Adi home and live out my ~~nightmarish~~ challenging life.

The only thing good that's come out of this meeting is her views about the change of school. Now, at least, I have something solid to back up my arguments. If only Krish would be open to seeing the doctor, with or without me, and getting an insight into the workings of his son's brain.

There has been a heavy downpour in the time we've been indoors. There's chaotic traffic coupled with aggressive honking. We'll have to cross the main road to get an autorickshaw. Adi's not moving, petrified of the vehicles coming from both sides. I have to literally drag him across. Another wait of ten minutes before we flag down an empty auto that's ready to take us home.

Check the phone—three messages.

> Don't forget to bring paneer on your way back. No delivery guys at our neighbourhood store and both Suryamani and I are doubling over with period pain. Love you, Jasmine.

Invariably, their monthly cycles overlap, not mine thankfully. Now I'd better get the paneer; otherwise, we'll have to settle for omelettes for the second day in a row.

> Please call when free.

Krish. This must be about the new school.

> How about lunch this Saturday?

Sreekumar. If only, let's see.

The rickshaw refuses to wait while I get the paneer, so Adi and I, completely drenched, trudge home under one umbrella. Adi hates the rain as much as I love it.

No surprise, the lift is not working again. Adi grumbles throughout our climb.

'Mom, you need to call Dad ASAP. It's urgent.' Jasmine's all over me before I enter the house.

'First, tell me how you are. And Suryamani? All okay?'

'Yeah, yeah, Mom, better.'

Adi scuttles into their bedroom and slams the door shut.

'Good, take the paneer and make me a cup of tea. What happened? Why did Dad call? Did he tell you anything?'

'OMG, I'm so excited! Dad's project has been extended. He's staying on in Mumbai for a couple more weeks. He's invited Adi and me to join them in Matheran for the long weekend this month. If you agree, he can book another room for us. Mom, please say yes! I've never been to Matheran and it will be such fun!'

'Can you stop pulling my cheeks, Jas? Let me find out the details, and then we'll see.'

Towelling his hair vigorously, Adi emerges from the bedroom demanding dinner. Dinner's going to be late tonight. He knows that, and yet he can't stand the change in routine.

I'd better call Krish. Never before has he taken the children anywhere. Since he moved to Singapore, soon after our divorce, he has never invited the children for a holiday. What's this sudden interest? Does he want to win them over and gain custody—not that he can without a long legal process? And anyway, Jas will legally be an adult very soon. His interest in Jas is understandable, but I'm pretty sure he'd not want to be saddled with Adi. Especially now that he's got another son.

Adi Krishnan

7

I don't know what all the fuss is about. Jas can't choose between two pairs of denim shorts. One's grey and the other blue. But both are shorts. She's all cut up about it.

'Tell me, baby brother, which one goes better with the red top?'

'The blue one,' says Suryamani. The question wasn't directed at her. But so what?

'You think so? But what about the grey?'

Mom enters our room. 'Jas, I can't seem to find my silver bracelet. Is it mixed with your accessories?'

Mom rifles through Jasmine's cupboard. I'm glad I'm the only male in the house. My stuff never gets mixed up with anyone else's. Mom, Jas and Suryamani are always looking for their belongings. Especially after laundry day.

'Mom, blue or grey?' Jas thrusts the shorts under Mom's nose.

'The blue, perhaps.'

'Fine. Sheesh Mom, your OOTD is simply fab!' Jas blows her a flying kiss.

'Thanks to Suryamani. She blow-dried my hair, almost strand by strand!'

'Strand by strand? Were you at it all morning, Mom?'

'Adi, sweetie, I don't mean it literally.'

Jas is right. Mom is looking pretty. Her hair is somehow fuller. It is falling straight down to her waist. Why is she so dressed up?

'Who's this Sreekumar? Are you going on a date, Mom?'

'C'mon, sweetie, it's just lunch with a colleague. Sreekumar's from the botany department. Don't you remember him, Adi? He's the guy who had come home once to drop my papers.'

'That lame, lanky guy?'

'I don't like your choice of words, Adi. Yes, he's got a slight limp because of his polio.'

'And he's single, Mom, and quite your type,' grins Jas.

'Very confusing. Need confirmation. It's a date— yes or no?'

'C'mon, Adi, give Mom a break. I'm just teasing her. She needs some adult company, doesn't she?'

'Where's the blessed bracelet? Never mind. I'll be late if I don't leave now.'

Suryamani taps Mom on the back. 'Aunty, don't forget to put on some lipstick.'

'Yes, thanks for the reminder. Bye, peeps. I'll be back in a couple of hours. Jas, be home latest by five, okay? And Adi, remember, you are going to help Suryamani with her English.'

Mom waves at us and leaves the room.

'Aunty, please take an umbrella. It's started to rain,' yells Suryamani.

'Really? The sky's clear actually,' Mom yells back.

Jas starts giggling. 'Mom, it's *naago varsaad*, as Mamaiji would say!'

'What's naago varsaad?' asks Suryamani, her eyebrows raised.

'Naked rain!'

'That's ridiculous. As though rain wears clothing, Jas!'

'Adi, don't take it literally. When it pours against a clear sky, we Parsis use this expression.'

'We are only half-Parsi!'

'Right, bro.' She gives me a high-five.

'You are going on a date, Jas?'

'Seriously, Adi, what can be farther from a date than this? We are a group of eight—guys and gals—going to watch a movie. That's all.'

'Including Sid?'

'Bet.'

With a toss of her ponytail, she flits into the bathroom to put on the blue shorts.

Different species of snakes moult between four and twelve times a year because their skin doesn't keep up with the growth of their bodies. It also gets rid of harmful parasites the skin may be carrying. Jas moults—gets rid of her wardrobe—once a year. But she's hardly growing any taller!

Suryamani says she will serve lunch as soon as Jas leaves. She wants to work on her English assignments. How utterly boring! I don't mind helping her in principle. But she takes so long with the exercises. Her spellings are atrocious. She prefers Jas as a tutor. But sometimes, I have to help her out.

Jas struts out, blowing flying kisses at me. On a pair of vertiginous heels. She leaves.

Suryamani brings me cabbage subzi and dal with two rotis.

L-U-N-C-H. Too grand a word. For last night's leftovers. But I like dal and roti.

The doorbell interrupts. Who else but Mandar?

'Sorry baba, forgot the house keys. Thank god, we keep a spare set with you!'

Nothing unusual. Happens at least once a week.

Suryamani goes into the kitchen to fetch his keys.

'How's school, baba? All well, I'm sure.'

Why does he call me baba? Because he can't remember my name? And why ask a question if he wants to answer it himself?

Mohit calls. He wants my help with the physics project. No problem. My project is ready already. I rattle off some ideas.

One hour of English grammar. Then Suryamani asks to be let off. She's pretending to be sleepy. Actually, she wants to watch TV.

Dad calls. 'Hi Adi. Where's Mom? She's not answering her cell.'

'She's out. It's not a date, Dad. It's just lunch with a colleague.'

'Oh, is that so? Well, not to worry, I'll call later.'

'Okay.'

'It's about the trip to Matheran. It's a hill station, so it may be chilly in the monsoon. I need to have a word with her about what you should pack.'

'Can I carry my books, Dad?'

'Sure. When are you going back to school, Adi?'

'Monday.'

'Oh, that's great. Best wishes, Adi.'

'Thanks, Dad. Bye.'

This Matheran business is bothering me. I don't want to go. I hate going anywhere. And now with Dad's new family. Just because Jas is keen, Mom says I have to tag along. Illogical. Unfair. Appalling.

Delna D. Krishnan

8

Oh shoot, when will they come? This waiting screws me up. I had already drunk two big cups of tea loaded with sugar. Suryamani goads me to take a nap. She says she'll wake me when they get here, but there's no way I can relax.

It was the call from the landlady this morning that ruined my day. She threatened to terminate the contract if I don't agree to pay the increased rent. We've been here for six years. It may not be the perfect apartment, but it's close to Adi's school, convenient for my commute, and not too far from Mummy's place. I don't want to move, but a fifteen per cent hike? ~~Criminal~~ Outrageous, to say the least! I don't think I'm going to share this news with anyone yet.

And then there was a call from Adi's school. Mummy's gone again.

At last the bell goes, making my stomach flutter a little more intensely.

The school bag is thrown to the floor. My pulse quickens; something's terribly wrong.

'Where's Jas? It's pizza night, Mom,' says Adi, coming up to me.

'Jas will be home anytime now. Pizza is once a month, Adi, and we had it a couple of weeks ago, didn't we?'

'I agree with Adi—it's definitely pizza night! And I'm going to treat you all to it,' smiles Mummy.

'Oh shoot, what's going on? A celebration? Am I missing something?'

'Mamaiji said to wait. But I'll burst if I don't tell you now. My physics project got the first prize in the inter-school competition, Mom!' The words rush out exuberantly, but his expression remains unchanged.

'Whoa! That's so ~~nice~~ fabulous to hear! I was so worried about your first day back to school. And that was why they called us?'

I reach out to hug my son, but he's gone.

'Felt good to hear some praise for Adi,' says Mummy. 'Incredibly good. Even Mrs Roberts made a mention of it.'

Adi returns with a glass of almond milk, munching a handful of roasted peanuts. Thank goodness he's adapted to almond milk. A member of the support group had suggested that limiting dairy could prove beneficial. It took a whole year for Adi to make the switch, but now he desists from touching even a drop of cow's milk.

'We have a new class teacher. Her name is Miss Blanche Rego. She says we should address her as Miss Blanche. Her subject is bio. She gave us a tough surprise test. Critical thinking MCQs and diagrams. I scored the highest!'

'I'm so proud of you, Adi!' I barely manage to tap him on the shoulder; he's grown so tall.

'There's a new girl in class. Tiny little thing. With two pigtails. Oriental features. We thought she's from China or Korea. But she's from Nagaland.'

'How interesting!'

'The teacher asked me to sit next to her. So that I can help her. There were some sneers. I didn't let that affect me.'

'Well done, Adi! Just don't take note of your nasty classmates and keep doing well.'

'Now I must complete my homework so that I can read later,' says Adi, leaving for his bedroom.

The smile doesn't leave my face. Aren't I lucky to have a son who loves doing his homework?

'I don't agree with what you are saying, Delna. He's got to learn to get along with his classmates. How long will you be able to protect him? He's got to adjust to the world outside or else he'll be eaten alive the moment he steps out of school, mark my words.'

Mummy scowls, wagging her finger to highlight the significance of her words.

'You are right, Mummy, but can we take one step at a time? In fact, I'm surprised that he's happy about the new teacher and the new student. Quite unlike him.'

Mummy rolls her eyes at me but mercifully holds her tongue.

Thank goodness the pizza is going to be sponsored; I'm not exactly feeling rich this month, plenty of unexpected expenses—what with a loan of twenty thousand for the repairs of Suryamani's village house and the gift of five thousand for Venky.

Our household hums with happiness for another hour as Mummy catches up with her daily soaps while I mark papers. Adi's down bicycling and Suryamani's chopping vegetables for tomorrow, which makes the mornings less hectic for her.

'Don't say I'm interfering, Delna, but poor Jasmine is quite desperate to get a tattoo done on the inside of her wrist.'

'Mummy, I know all about it. She's mentioned it a few times but I don't think it's appropriate at all.'

'I can't say I'm in favour of it, but she was telling me all her friends have them and—'

'I remember how she inveigled me into getting the second piercing done in both ears. If she thinks you can twist my arm, she's mistaken. And she wants a S; no marks for guessing why!'

'Really? She told me it's going to be a vine.'

'Quite right, an S-shaped vine. Besides, her skin is sensitive, Mummy. I don't want more problems than I can handle. Can we enjoy the evening for once and not take up contentious issues?'

Mummy nods and lets it go for the moment. Thank goodness! She spends the next half an hour in the kitchen getting to know the latest about Suryamani's family.

Jasmine floats in, joy unbounded, because she hasn't flunked the maths exam. And then she celebrates her brother's success with squeals of delight and war cries. How did these two kids, so totally unlike each other, emerge from the same womb? My precious munchkins!

Finally, I allow myself to stretch, release the tense muscles and lie down on the sofa, which feels good after the anxiety of the day. Looking at my children and their grandmother, arguing about the pizza toppings and how many pizzas to order, brings a smile to my face. My children and Mummy are the glue that holds me together, and makes me want to continue living and believing in a better future.

I must call Krish later tonight and let him know about Adi's brilliant performance. Adi may not be socially adept, but the child is gifted; there's no doubt about it. And his dad needs to acknowledge the boy's strengths. And the school isn't all bad, as I keep saying.

The doorbell propels both the children to the door to grab the parcel. No, it's not the delivery man, I can hear H&M at the door.

As I sit up and straighten my hair, they walk in with an adorable brown pup in Mandar's arms.

'Hey Delna, meet Zeba!'

Thrilled to bits, Jasmine pleads with Mandar to hand Zeba to her.

'She's asleep, Jasmine. But you can play with her every day, I promise,' says Harish.

'She's just a week old now. You can take her for a walk when she grows bigger,' adds Mandar.

'Man, I've wanted a dog for so long! Isn't this amazing, Mom?'

'Yes, such a cutie! Where did you guys get her from? What breed is she?'

'You know, Delna, that shelter for strays where we volunteer? Zeba's pregnant mother was brought in bleeding with deep gashes. She had been stoned by some cruel buggers—excuse the language—and the vet had to perform an emergency caesarean. Her mother died soon after and . . . four pups were up for adoption. We couldn't help but bring one home,' says Harish.

'That's very nice, but who will look after her all day?' asks Mummy.

'I'm going to work from home for a few days,' says Mandar. 'Let's see, we'll sort it out by and by.'

Except Adi, all of us fuss over tiny Zeba curled up in Mandar's hands. Adi stands away from all of us, in a corner, visibly upset. Fortunately, nobody else notes his lack of enthusiasm.

When the men leave, the pizza arrives, and my children swoop down on the goodies. Fast food is not particularly nutritious, but what the heck? Once in a while, we can afford to indulge ourselves, can't we? We are only human.

The pup is forgotten; our energies are diverted to dividing up the two big pizzas, sprinkling the oregano and chilli flakes on each slice, with massive gobs of ketchup and buttery garlic bread on the side. Our 'oohs' and 'aahs' fade as the food flies off our plates. Determined to pamper us further, Mummy orders kulfi and the house resounds with 'thank you, Mamaiji', our Coke cans raised to salute her generosity.

Adi Krishnan

9

Struggling. To keep my cool. Very tough.

It is less than two days since I returned to school. The class is back to their nasty ways. Name-calling. Teasing. Endless.

I try to remember Dr Parekh's words: 'Ignore them. Don't take the bait.'

I'm quiet. Teeth clenched. Weapons of Mass Destruction, aka pencils, sharpened.

Miss Blanche gave each student a different article from *Sanctuary* magazine. After some time, she asks everyone to stop reading. She asks us to share one interesting fact.

I am still reading.

Riya is going on about the dodo's closest living relative being the Nicobar pigeon. Miss Blanche stops her and asks me how to prevent extinction.

'You have interrupted my train of thought, miss.'

The class breaks into laughter. What now? I haven't said anything wrong, have I?

Miss Blanche quietens them with a movement of her hands. She says sorry to me. I don't need an apology. I just want to make it clear that I'm not done reading yet.

'I haven't decided what I want to share,' I add. 'There are five interesting facts and five well-known facts about the armadillo that I've gathered so far.'

Miss Blanche asks me to share one fact from each category.

The class titters some more. For no reason. Her brusque reprimand shuts them up.

Everyone knows that armadillos are native to North, South and Central America. I'm kind of surprised that the nine-banded armadillo gives birth to identical quadruplets every time.

She asks me why that's surprising.

Because it's a one-in-a-million chance for human beings to have identical quadruplets.

'I want you to learn from Adi how to classify information and how to build your reasoning ability,' says Miss Blanche to the class.

What's so great about what I've just said? That's the only way to think, isn't it?

The laughter halts. I suppose I should enjoy the moment.

During the break, Shakeel and Mohit walk past my desk. Shakeel whispers something to Mohit.

Mohit responds loudly. 'Of course. Weirdo, armadillo!'

I count to ten and take a deep breath. By then, Mohit and Shakeel have left the class.

Riya invites Suzila, the new girl, to sit with Ankita and her gang on the staircase facing our classroom. Suzila takes her lunchbox and goes out. She's back on her own in a couple of minutes.

'Eaten already?' I ask.

'No.' She shakes her head. Her pigtails bob up and down.

'Why not?'

'I have chicken sandwiches. Riya says I can't sit with her group because they are vegetarians.'

'You can eat them here. No problem.'

'Really? Do you eat chicken?'

'Yes, I love chicken sandwiches.'

Suzila shares her sandwich with me. I really like it. Massive chunks of chicken slathered with mayo between two slices of multigrain bread. She likes my chutney-tomato sandwich. I tell her she can eat with me every day of school.

She keeps smiling at me. I hope she doesn't want to be my girlfriend. Jas and Sid share samosa-chai daily.

After break, Shakeel and Mohit walk straight to me and Suzila.

'Armadillo's made a new friend, Mohit,' says Shakeel.

'New friend? You mean *only* friend, Shakeel,' responds Mohit, laughing.

'And please note, it's a girl,' adds Shakeel in a high-pitched voice.

'That's hardly surprising. He's not man enough to have guy friends,' says Mohit, slapping Shakeel on the back.

'*Kya sahi bola, bhai,*' laughs Shakeel.

'Shut up. Not a word more from you two sickos,' I say, getting up, 'or I'll have to report you both to Miss Blanche.'

'What else can you do!' says Mohit. He laughs even more. Both move to the back of the class.

After the break, it's English class. Mrs Rao announces the marks of the weekly dictation test. Besides me, Shakeel and Rosie also get twenty out of twenty. The class jeers at Suzila who gets the lowest score, four out of twenty. Mrs Rao tries to quieten everyone. Nobody listens to her.

Each one is asked to read aloud a paragraph from the Rapid Reader. Mrs Rao comments. She tells me the same thing each time—*monotonous, too fast*. I've never understood why she bothers. Riya and Mohit are appreciated. For their perfect intonation. Their perfect expression. Their confidence.

Suzila can hardly read. She fumbles with almost every word. Even Suryamani reads far better.

Suzila speaks well. Why is her reading so messed up? Could her brain be less developed, like a reptile's?

The last class. PE. My most hated class. I excuse myself. I have a stomach ache. The teacher insists that I go to the playground. Not the library.

The noise from the construction work. In the neighbouring plot. Deafening. The teacher has to scream out instructions. The class is asked to do warm-ups. Then jog five times around the playground. They do the warm-ups. Then protest that they would like to play kho-kho. The teacher relents. The violent game begins. So glad I'm just a spectator.

Suzila is targeted. But she plays like a pro. She defends herself well, and she tags the greatest number of opponents! Hers is the winning team. Her captain, Mohit, thumps her on the back. The whole team claps for her.

We return to the school building. Suzila walks beside me. Her chocolatey-golden pigtails jiggle up and down.

'Are you feeling better, Adi? Wish you had joined us. I've had such a great time!'

'Shall I tell you the truth? I don't have a stomach ache. PE freaks me out so I have to invent some or the other story every time!'

'Really? You are so good at everything, Adi, I thought—'

'My coordination is no good, my mom says. And the doctor concurs.'

I look all around to see if anyone heard me use the word 'doctor'.

Mom says I must not mention to anyone that I see a psychiatrist. But sharing it with Suzila doesn't seem so bad.

'The doctor tells me I'm too delicate. And that I must limit my physical activities, but I don't listen to him at all. So don't worry too much about what your doctor says, Adi.'

She stretches her arm out to me. I quicken my strides. Where's the need to touch? That, too, after a game of kho-kho? Her hands are full of germs from touching others and falling to the ground.

Shirin Ardeshir Daruwala

10

Never mind that I'm missing the yoga class; Jas and Sid are coming over for a cooking demo on bhakra. I really don't understand why Adi has to accompany them. But my daughter has made up her mind to send him along, and I couldn't talk her out of it.

Sid is coming to my place for the first time. I've made sure the house is tip-top, not that it's ever untidy but still. He must know—we may not be wealthy people but we have class. And Dadar Parsi Colony, centrally located, is a much sought after address because of its peaceful locale.

I've kept all the ingredients out—wheat flour, semolina, brown sugar, eggs, ghee, powdered almonds-nutmeg-cardamom, and for me the most important ingredient, toddy. I don't want to waste time measuring stuff when they arrive. They must be tired coming right after college; I've got cheese sandwiches and chocolate milkshakes ready for the in-between time when we wait for the fermentation action of the toddy to make the dough rise. Many people nowadays use yoghurt and baking powder instead of toddy, but not me. I believe in following our traditional recipes with the most authentic ingredients.

I'm ready and waiting by 2 p.m.—they are expected at about 3 p.m. Rather than taking a nap, I sit in the armchair in my veranda. My eyes can't help admiring the pocket-sized garden. My rose bushes and my hibiscus plant are the pride of the colony. So grateful to Ardeshir for choosing this ground-floor flat. I wanted a higher floor, but he had convinced me that we could avail of the garden if we were on the ground floor. And now, with my knees being what they are, it seems to have been the wisest decision.

'Mamaiji, open the door. We're here!' Jas announces their arrival in her musical voice and at the same time, rat-a-tats on my door. If Naju has heard the ruckus, she's sure to sprint down, despite the bunions on her feet, to find out what's going on.

'Welcome Sid! It's your first time here, isn't it?' I clasp him in a tight embrace, and he returns it warmly. Tall and lean, he's got a dazzling smile.

They drop their rucksacks on the floor like teenagers do. Jas is all over me, as usual. Adi troops in after them.

'Yes, Mamaiji, thank you for inviting me,' says Sid in his rich baritone as he sits down on my ancient rosewood sofa. These days, you won't find such mild-mannered boys, even if you go out looking for them with searchlights.

Adi's greeting comes in the form of a question in his mechanical voice. 'Why did we have to come here and cook?'

'You didn't have to, Adi. It was Jasmine's idea.' I hope he's not going to spoil the afternoon with his wisecracks.

'I agree with Adi, Mamaiji,' laughs Sid. 'I love eating your bhakras, but cooking is an entirely different matter! My dad enjoys it, not me. Did you know Mamaiji, my dad makes the best sorpotel in the whole of Goa?' Crossing his legs, he flashes one more suave, relaxed smile. *Ghanoj mittho chhe!*

'Adi, what say? How about you and me watching a documentary on snakes? Shall we?' says Sid, mischief in his eyes.

'I've seen all the documentaries that exist if you're talking of Nat Geo. I doubt I'll learn anything more, but thanks for your offer, Sid,' says Adi, missing the joke completely.

Jasmine protests, 'Man, I wanna kill you, didn't you say—'

'Hey, peace, now that we're here, we shall go through the ordeal, Jas! What say, Adi?'

Adi looks perplexed. 'I have nothing to say.'

Jas slaps Sid on the back, and he raises his arms in mock surrender. Their youth, their vitality and their sizzling banter warms my heart. A good marriage is based on friendship first and foremost, like mine was; that's what gives it a solid foundation. I can already see these two friends walking down the aisle in a Goan church. I'd better rein in my thoughts. There's a task waiting to be accomplished.

'Relax, you and Adi don't have to actually do anything,' I add quickly. 'You can sit and watch the demo. Would you like a cold drink before we begin?'

'Why are we wasting time, Mamaiji? Let's get on with it,' goes Adi, the perpetual grump. 'I have to go home and complete my revision.' He's shifting from one foot to the other.

'Yes, Mamaiji. Let's begin,' says Sid.

'Everything's ready. Come to the kitchen. Sid, it's not a grand kitchen, just a simple one,' I add.

The boy ignores my remark. I don't think he really cares what my house looks like. Jas is all he cares about.

The three of them follow me, and I point out the items that will go into creating the bhakra. Jas is taking notes on her phone.

'Which is wheat flour? And which is semolina?' Adi edges closer to the two chinaware platters standing side by side. The one with semolina is pushed over the edge of the counter with a nudge from his elbow. The china shatters; the bits and pieces mixed with the semolina are strewn over my freshly cleaned kitchen.

'Adi, how can you be so careless? I wish you had stayed home. Get away from the counter before you cause any more damage!' I look away, gnashing my teeth in frustration. No one can get under my skin like Adi does, except his mother, of course.

'It's not my fault. It just happened, Mamaiji.' He takes a step or two back, guilt showing in his eyes.

'Dhoor ne dhefar. Not your fault!'

'Chill, Mamaiji, we'll clear the mess, not to worry,' says Jas. She's so damn protective of her brother. Always.

Jasmine gets the mop, Sid takes it from her hands and deftly collects the remains, locates the dustbin and in one smooth move, disposes of the remains.

'It's not just about clearing the mess. I've run out of semolina. That's the last I had.'

'Can't we do without it . . . or use something else instead?' says quick-thinking Sid.

'No, Sid, unfortunately, we can't make bhakra without it.'

'Not to worry, Mamaiji. Adi and I will buy some more from the corner shop. That won't take long.'

Jas disappears with her brother before I can react. Smart girl, she wants to remove him from the scene of the crime. I have no option but to cool down.

'Come, Sid, let's sit and wait for their return. Will you have some Pepsi?'

'No aerated drinks for me, Mamaiji. Water will do.'

We go back to the living room with our glasses of chilled water. We make small talk about his family, their farm in Goa and their two Alsatians.

'Sid, what's your career plan? Are you going to follow in your parents' footsteps? Become a doctor?'

'Oh no, not me. I'm going to be an architect or perhaps a musician.'

'Wow, architect sounds good. Music, you can pursue as a hobby, no?'

'Let's see, Mamaiji. Not sure yet.'

'Even Jas is not sure what she's going to do after the twelfth,' I say, looking at him out of the corner of my eyes.

'Jas should pursue anything other than science. Her heart is not in it.' His snicker doesn't give anything away.

I suppose Delna is right. They are too young now, and if they go their separate ways, god knows what will happen in the future . . .

The brother-sister duo returns.

'Sorry, Mamaiji.' Adi hands the packet to me. His sister must have coached him to offer an apology.

'Just learn to be careful, *dikra*. I never scold you without a reason—it's for your own good.'

Sheepish, he nods.

'Cheer up, bro. It could have easily been any of us. My mom calls me butterfingers!' says Sid.

Jas and I laugh. I cannot imagine Sid ever being clumsy or ungainly. It's one more of his endearing traits—that he's always nice to Adi.

We return to the kitchen. The work progresses without any untoward incident. Jas and Sid take turns to knead the dough, and Adi lurks in the background for a while before disappearing to the living room. He must be reading his book; what else?

While we wait for the toddy to do its magic, they enjoy my snacks. Sid and Jas entertain me with songs and jokes. Half the time I don't understand their lingo, but I join in the merriment. The boy does sing well. Mark my words, he could become a famous singer.

Sid and Jas insist on frying the bhakras themselves. I show them how to do a couple, and then they take over. The bhakras turn out crisp on the outside and soft and creamy inside, as is ideal. Sid can't stop praising me and my craft. I pack a dozen for his family and a dozen for mine, leaving just three or four for myself. No big deal, I can always make a fresh batch.

'Mamaiji, now allow me to wash the dishes and do the general clean-up. My mom says I'm pretty good at it,' says Sid, raising his collar.

'I'm sure you are, Sid. But thanks; my helper will be coming. You all carry on, but promise me that you will come again!'

'I will, Mamaiji, if you promise it's not going to be one more cookery class!'

He winks at me and I wink back, while Jas lands another hard slap on his back.

They leave. Adi appears to be contrite; I don't know if it's a pretence or if he is genuinely so.

Chalo, I'm not going to let it all wait until my helper comes tomorrow morning. I'll get to work, can't stand dirty dishes in the sink. And the floor will have to be thoroughly mopped; I don't want ants crawling in my kitchen.

Two things that give me sleepless nights are red ants and seepage. In my kitchen, there's a moist patch on the ceiling; Naju insists that everything is fine in her flat, but I have my doubts. Shall have to call the plumber and if required, get the work done. Naju had better be ready to split the expenses, no *kat-kat*.

Jasmine Krishnan

II

Why do I always have to make choices? Mom says I'm really lucky to have to choose between two good options, but honestly, this has been a hard decision. I feel real FOMO, man.

We have just checked into the hotel in Matheran, and I'm over the moon about spending a weekend with Dad. At the same time, I am wondering if I should have gone to Goa with Sid and his parents. This is the first time they invited me, and Mom didn't mind my joining them, but it happened to be the exact same weekend as Dad's offer. What could I have done, man? Sid's promised to share pictures every hour on the hour, but it's not the same, is it?

Venky and I have really hit it off. He slept through most of the car ride from Mumbai. When he was awake, he played peek-a-boo with me and even preferred my shoulder to Geetha's for an hour or so. When we got to the point where we had to park the car and walk the rest of the way, Geetha and Venky got into the cycle rickshaw with all the luggage while the three of us soldiered on. I don't have anything against Geetha, but lacing my fingers through Dad's, our footsteps treading the red soil with the sun's weak rays breaking through the tops of trees, just the three of us, felt special and so right.

Adi was quiet throughout our journey. I was glad. He doesn't like going to new places. As a kid, he would throw tantrums any time we tried to go on vacation, so we never did. I also hated it when, in new places, people who did not know him, treated him as if he were dim. My brother is smarter than all of you, I would want to yell.

Mom gave Adi many lectures on being well-behaved before we left. I don't think Mom will sleep a wink. She's so worried about Adi. Man, I'm so glad she's going out with her colleagues, though—that will help her relax. Unfortunately, Sreekumar's on a trek, so he won't be part of the dinner party. I don't know him at all, but if they get closer and it makes Mom happier, I'm all for it. Fingers crossed, as Mamaiji and I often tell each other.

As soon as we get into our room and unpack, Adi begins to whine. He's forgotten to bring along his smelly old *razai*, the quilt he's had since he was a year old. Mom doesn't wash it often because she's worried it will fall apart. He's also disturbed by the persistent cricket noises that have begun to get louder as the evening light slips away.

'Jas, I won't get any sleep tonight,' he says for the umpteenth time.

I love him to death, but Adi can be annoying at times, and this is one of those times.

There's a knock. Geetha pops her head in and asks us to head to the dining room for dinner. I tell her we'll be down shortly.

'What are we going to eat, Jas?' asks Adi.

'How do I know, Adi? Just shut up and eat whatever is served, okay?'

Now I'm stressed about Adi. I hope he does not refuse to eat. He does that sometimes when the food is something he has never had before.

We wend our way to the spacious dining room with big French windows. There's another family seated by one of the windows and a loved-up couple in the corner below the staircase.

'Hope you've freshened up, children. We ordered chicken biryani and paneer kofta. Do you like that, children? And ice cream for dessert,' says Dad.

'Is there coriander in the kofta? Jas won't eat it then,' spouts my not-so-tactful brother.

'Really? Sorry, I didn't know this, Jas. We can inform the kitchen . . . for tomorrow,' says Geetha.

'It's okay, aunty. I can just push it aside.' My face reddens.

'Why do you call her "aunty"? She's our dad's wife and—'

Before Adi can put his foot deeper into his mouth, I search for something sensible to say! Geetha beats me to it.

'Call me anything you like, Adi. Geetha's fine as well,' she says, running her hands through his hair.

Adi bristles. He can't stand anyone touching him, least of all people he doesn't know well.

'Shall I call you stepmom, then?' asks Adi. Man, the foot has almost disappeared in his mouth.

'That's not a very nice term, kanna.' Dad sends him a killer look.

'Why not, Krish? Technically, it's the right term, Adi. It's the connotation that we give to this term that spoils it,' Geetha interjects with a smile.

Seated in his highchair, Venky starts going 'da-da-da' and everyone's attention is diverted. Thankfully.

The food arrives, and the spicy, tangy aroma gets us all drooling. Adi does not reject it. The kofta's buried under coriander, but I manage to dig the paneer out. Yummy! The biryani couldn't be better.

'What does Venky call you?' Adi looks at Geetha, the challenge showing in his eyes.

'Nothing as yet. But I would like him to call me Amma.'

Geetha reaches out to Venky and tweaks his cheeks, kissing him on the forehead.

'Adi, please call her aunty. That will be the right thing,' insists Dad, shushing Geetha who begins to protest.

'I'll think about it. Shall let you know in the morning,' says unflappable Adi.

Everyone's having their fill of chocolate ice cream. Venky's mouth and fingers are smeared with the gooey stuff as he keeps dipping his fingers into the bowl. Geetha and I feed him a spoonful in turn.

Geetha fetches a Scrabble board. My brother excels, as expected. Adi wins five of the six rounds and Dad's chest swells with pride. He tells us that he used to be a Scrabble champ in his teens.

We then play *antakshari*. Geetha's trained in classical music, and I don't sing too badly myself, so we have to be in opposite teams. Dad and Adi make half-hearted attempts to join in, but it's only Geetha and I who are really interested. The session ends quite lamely, and we call it a night.

Geetha hugs and kisses us good night, much to Adi's horror. He wipes off her kisses, which is not noticed by her. Thankfully.

When we are back in our room, I tell him to drop the stepmom business.

'Geetha's awfully sweet, isn't she, Adi?'

'Sweet like payasam?'

'Very funny, Adi. I'm not amused. Don't you like her though?'

'I guess so. Have you noticed her face, Jas?'

'What do you mean?'

'She's got a terraced face.'

'What's a terraced face?'

'Yeah, from her forehead to her chin, she's got levels like a terraced field.'

'Seriously, I don't know where you get these ideas from, Adi! She's nice looking, and more importantly, she's being very nice to us. She gave us the largest helpings of ice cream, if you noticed, Adi.'

'Maybe she doesn't care for ice cream, Jas.'

'Oh, stop it, Adi!'

Adi begins grumbling about the missing razai.

Ignoring him, I busy myself scrolling through pictures of Sid—on the beach, swimming, eating jumbo shrimp and generally having a good time. Can't call him now; he's out partying with his cousins.

Mom calls to find out how we are; I tell her that we are doing fine.

Adi asks me to leave the bathroom light on because he's scared of the dark in a strange place.

'Jas, Jas, get up. I can't sleep, there's a lizard.'

Man, it's 2 a.m. and I'm being shaken awake by my brother. I wanna throttle him.

'Where's the lizard?'

Through half-closed eyes, I see an innocent baby lizard high up on the wall.

'What am I supposed to do, Adi? Go back to sleep, for god's sake.'

With the sheet pulled over my face, I try to shut out Adi's whines as well as the cricket noises.

Jasmine Krishnan

12

Man, I'm so hungry. I head to the dining room before anyone else.

The breakfast buffet is just the kind I like. There's idli, coconut chutney, fried eggs, cornflakes and fruit.

The dreaded Matheran monkeys are looking at the food through the French windows. The manager had already warned us that they could be very aggressive.

Geetha, Venky and Dad arrive. After Venky's installed in the highchair, Dad starts talking about what we're going to do this morning.

Adi comes down last, greets us all and says to Geetha, 'Good morning, Geethamma. That's your new name.'

Dad almost drops his cup of coffee! He starts thumping the table. 'That's perfect, Adi! What do you say, Geetha?'

'Good morning, Adi. I really like my new name!' says Geetha, who's been feeding idli to Venky. She flashes a bright smile at Adi and makes the victory sign.

'I couldn't have found a better term myself!' says Dad. 'Adi, you're a genius, kanna. What say, Jas?'

'Yes, Dad; she's Geethamma for me as well now. Better than aunty, for sure.'

Pleased with the praise coming his way, Adi starts quizzing us about—what else—snakes. None of us can answer him correctly because he's armed with obscure facts. How many grams of venom from a death adder are enough to kill a human being? The answer is twenty grams. As if we cared. None of us are likely to encounter a death adder or a cottonmouth anytime soon. For someone who can't tolerate a harmless house lizard, I don't understand his interest in—of all things—venomous snakes.

Without a whimper of warning, Venky starts crying at full volume. He is loud enough to make the other family look in our direction and make the manager come running to our table.

'He must have soiled his nappy. Not to worry, folks. I'll be back in a jiffy.' Dad jumps up, picks up Venky, and starts walking towards the staircase.

'Thanks, love,' coos Geethamma, as she spreads the marmalade on Adi's toast.

I rise to ask Dad if he needs my help, but my cool stepmom motions for me to stay in my seat.

'Your dad can manage quite well, Jas, don't ruin your breakfast! And that's how it should be, right? Dads must be fully involved in bringing up their children,' she says.

Geethamma goes on to tell us how they divvy up the chores at home. I can't recall Dad doing any housework when he lived with us! I can't help but feel a little jealous of their idyllic lives. I mean, Mom does her best and we're happy as we are. But we aren't a complete fam.

Dad returns with Venky and attacks his breakfast again with gusto. Venky's smiling and babbling happily.

'I haven't gone to the bathroom yet. What about your bowel movements? Jas? Dad? Geethamma?' Adi's finger flags each one of us in turn.

Honestly, when is Adi gonna understand that some topics are off-limits?!

'It's not something to be discussed, especially at the breakfast table, Adi,' Dad says. Sharply.

'Why not? At home, we do,' says Adi. Defiant.

Dad says, 'That's okay but—'

'I know we can't discuss things like stools and farting and such with anyone but one's family. So aren't we a family?' Adi asks. Genuinely.

'Yes, we are family. To answer your question, Adi, I've done the big job this morning. Hope you too can relieve yourself so that you can eat well,' Geethamma responds, handing him his toast. Got to give it to her; she's one hell of a woman!

Before Dad can continue to reprimand Adi, Venky throws up. Bits of half-digested idli fly and settle on Geethamma and me, who are nearest. Venky's cries grow louder as more yellow stuff dribbles out. Yuck. I move away as fast as I can.

The monkeys are now banging on the windows. My brother sidles up to me, saying he's scared. Will they attack us? Will we have to get rabies shots? I quell his fears with a firm 'no'.

Dad and Geethamma are trying to calm Venky, whose face is turning as red as the monkeys' backsides.

'I think he's feverish, love. I better stay back this morning. Why don't you all go for a nice walk?' Geethamma says to Dad.

Dad and I protest that Venky will be fine, but Geethamma stands her ground.

'Fine. Jas and Adi, let's leave in half an hour.'

'No, Dad, I'll stay behind with Geethamma. Why don't you and Adi go?'

Geethamma coaxes me to join them, but I'm equally determined to stay with her.

'Where are we going, Dad?' asks Adi.

'How about the Panorama point?'

Adi nods and the father and son set off shortly afterwards, both wielding walking sticks. Adi likes walking and being outdoors. I am sure he will be fine.

We go to their room. Venky naps and Geethamma and I chat like friends. She yaks about her college days; I tell her about my girl gang . . . and Sid, of course. No cap, my decision to stay back with her was so right.

Because I can trust her, I tell her that Adi doesn't like to be touched. At once, she becomes more closely attentive, and she asks me to tell her anything else that she should know about Adi. I tell her not to mind some of the things he says. Kissing me on the forehead, she calls me 'the world's best sister'.

Watching the antics of the monkeys who are so good at making off with people's parcels—they seem to zero in on the women—makes the tears stream down my cheeks. We laugh a lot, eat chocolate and play with Venky when he awakes.

Dad and Adi return in high spirits, never mind that their clothes are mud-splattered. Adi shows us the pics of spectacular views of the Western Ghats. Dad keeps patting Adi because it was Adi who stopped him from falling at one point. I can't believe it because generally Adi's the one with the awkward moves.

Bathed and changed, Adi can't stop talking about Dad. Especially how Dad warded off the monkeys with a lion-like growl and banging of the stick. Pizza and pav bhaji for lunch turn us into an even merrier group. There's watermelon for dessert. Both Geethamma and I burst into Harry Styles' 'Watermelon Sugar', keeping the beat with our feet, and soon we are up dancing away. The other family begins clapping and whistling, cheering us on, and the young couple matches our steps. Except for my brother, who looks away, everyone's having a gala time.

No news from Sid; he must be asleep after last night's partying. Even though it's a little corny, I send him a haiku that I've composed:

Primeval forests
Misty trees and grassy hills
No path leads to you!

I talk to Mom and tell her what a great time we are having. Mamaiji calls. She wants to know if Geethamma is treating us badly. Seriously, this notion of 'stepmoms' is so antiquated that it should remain within the pages of fairy tales.

After a short afternoon siesta, we are off to Charlotte Lake. Dad leads the way with Venky up on his shoulders. Geethamma and I march hand in hand, singing along with the songs from my playlist. Adi brings up the rear because he's stopping to see the clumps of wildflowers and mushrooms growing along our path. I think he's really worried that one of the venomous snakes may pop out from somewhere.

The walk is unforgettable. The path is misty and dreamy under the trees. We sit by the water, munching peanuts. Dad tells us about his childhood; none of us had heard those stories before.

Adi reminds us to start back before sunset so that we can return to the security of the hotel before nightfall. In the fading light, we make our way, with Dad and Adi marching ahead. It starts drizzling and instantly the weather turns chilly. Geethamma stops to put on Venky's sweater and hat. She and I link arms to keep each other warm.

After dinner, I'm rocking Venky to sleep when Sid calls. Quickly, I deposit Venky in Dad's arms and go into the courtyard where Sid and I exchange anecdotes non-stop for an hour or so.

On my return to our room, I find Adi sitting on his bed, staring at nothing in particular, looking crestfallen.

'I'm feeling sad too, Adi. Tomorrow we return to Mumbai, and a couple of days later, Dad will be flying back to Singapore.'

'That's not what I'm thinking. Mom should have been here,' he says. 'When I see Geethamma sitting with us, I wish I could wipe her out and copy-paste Mom instead. Don't you, Jas?'

This thought hadn't struck me, but he's so right! Geethamma's great in every way, but she's not Mom. While my brother may not be able to verbalize the thought of missing Mom in so many words, he does it in his inimitable Adi-style.

Honestly, I never want him to change. His direct matter-of-fact approach is so much better than regular guys who can be scheming, devious and hypocritical. Even Sid's quite fond of Adi; he thinks Adi's a bit goofy, yet he's full of admiration for his intellect and his infinite capacity for remembering facts, even the trivial ones.

'Jas, do you know why Dad left Mom?'

'It's not like Dad left Mom or Mom left Dad ... they weren't happy together, so they decided to go their separate ways, that's all.'

'Were they fighting all the time? Do you remember? You were older when they split.'

'I was just seven, Adi. I really don't remember much.'

'Why does Mom still wear her wedding ring?'

'That's not her wedding band, Adi. That's a diamond ring gifted by Mamaiji on her wedding day. Adi, let's not ruin our holiday by digging into the past. It's water under the bridge, anyway.'

I hug my brother and video call Mom, giving her a lowdown on the day.

Delna D. Krishnan

13

Oh shoot, almost got into an auto, forgetting that autos don't ply to Dadar. Suryamani left for her village to help with her sister-in-law's delivery, so we had no option but to move to my childhood home for some days. To say the least, my commute is going to be ~~very annoying~~ far more expensive for the next few days. Jas is obviously very excited, and Adi doesn't mind it because we do spend weekends there now and then. Thank goodness!

Actually, I'm more than pleased with Adi—the weekend in Matheran was incident-free. Both Krish and Geetha went on about how much they loved having the kids, insisting they would like them to visit Singapore during the summer vacation.

When the taxi enters Dadar Parsi Colony, a sense of calm descends on me immediately. It's an oasis in

Mumbai—with green tree-lined avenues—that I took for granted while growing up. All the memories of Ruzbeh and me cycling, climbing trees and bruising our knees crowd my head. The cries of fish vendors, always women; the back-and-forth bargaining; the exchange of curses; the cycle bell of the weekly mutton-wala—two trings meant he was carrying a goat's brain, and you had to be quick to lay claim to it before it was snapped up by sharp-eyed Naju or anyone else.

Spending my formative years here was both comforting and claustrophobic. Comforting because everybody knew everybody and claustrophobic for the same reason. Once I went to college, I discovered a big, wide world beyond the colony, beyond the community, but it's super nice to be back for a few days. And this time it's going to be kind of extra special because of the ten days of *muktad*, followed by the Parsi New Year.

Being in a Parsi colony at this time provides a great sense of belonging. Every home gets spruced up for the new year. Sandalwood and incense smoke wafting from almost every flat, the scent of flowers mixed with the aroma of delicacies, the chalk patterns outside each home, the exchange of *sev* and *ravo* on New Year's Day . . . I wouldn't miss it for anything.

Mummy will be her most pious self during these days, murmuring prayers constantly with her head bowed and covered with a headscarf at all times. It's her way of connecting with my dad, whom she misses terribly. After Dad's passing, she's refashioned her life admirably, doing yoga, going on nature walks and of course, supporting me substantially. What would I do without her?

Her flat is on the ground level. I see her and my kids through the window. Jas lets me in.

Bending down to hug her, I marvel at Mummy's energy levels at seventy. I doubt I'll be able to do half as much when I'm her age, assuming that I live that long.

'Mummy, the house looks spotless!'

'Man, don't miss the new curtains,' says Jas, drawing out the white lacy drapes with tiny yellow tulips scattered all over the fabric.

'As though my house is ever dirty, Delna.' Mummy pouts, faking indignation.

'C'mon, you know what I mean, Mummy.' I pout back at her and settle into the easy chair. The house is redolent of the white-and-green tuberoses as well as the mild perfume of tiny baby-pink roses whose petals fall apart at the gentlest touch, unlike the larger decorative roses that lack fragrance.

'With the support of my part-time help and a heavy dose of painkillers, I've managed to clean the house from top to bottom. Every nook and cranny swept and swabbed, every pot, every pan shining,' Mummy says.

'Mamaiji, you could have waited for us to come and help you,' says Jas.

'Thanks; no need. Now the house is fit for Ardeshir and all our ancestors; they will be most pleased with the reception and shower us with their blessings before their departure on New Year's Eve.' Mummy smiles, smoothing out her white pleated skirt and hand-embroidered white blouse.

'This is all hogwash,' says my son. 'I don't believe. In god. It's a man-made belief system.'

'You can believe whatever you want, Adi, but while you are here, you will respect my wishes and follow our traditions,' responds Mummy, still holding on to her beatific smile.

'I agree with Mamaiji, Adi. Honouring our forefathers is customary in every civilization,' I add.

Nosy Naju pops in to see the preparations for muktad. She makes a few perfunctory remarks about how happy she is to see us, but soon reveals the real reason for coming. She wants a taste of Mummy's famed *malido*. Mummy informs her that she will share it only after the rituals begin tomorrow. Naju also wants to know if Mummy has bought sandalwood for the holy fire and how much it costs.

'Sandalwood is prohibitively expensive, as you know, Naju, but I'm not the one to cut corners. Nowadays, people don't seem to mind spending lavishly on designer clothes and fancy restaurants but crib about how expensive sandalwood is—dhoor ne dhefar! I'd readily sacrifice a trip to a foreign country rather than scrimp on my traditions,' says Mummy with her head held high.

Advantage, Mummy! That remark about foreign trips pricks Naju big time. She changes the topic quickly.

'Adi, you can come up to see the cobra snakeskin that my son-in-law brought from the jungles of Madhya Pradesh whenever you like. I know you're fond of snakes,' she says.

'Aunty, do you know what your name has in common with cobras?' Oh shoot, I hope he's not going to say something rude.

'My name?' Naju looks nonplussed.

'Yes, the scientific name of a cobra is Naja naja. Close to your name, right?'

'I didn't know that, Adi. You're really brainy, dikra.' Naju smiles weakly before making a quick exit.

After a light dinner of *turiya-par-eeda*, Jas retires to Mummy's bedroom. Adi and I share my childhood room. I wish Ruzbeh could have been here . . . haven't seen him for almost five years.

Every day for the next ten days, Mummy will get up at 4 a.m. and go to the agiary after a purifying bath. Then she will make breakfast for us while I get our tiffins ready for school and college. In the afternoon, she will make another trip to the agiary. Thank goodness, the agiary is a mere five minutes away. I resolve to try to visit the agiary most evenings before we both fix dinner.

Blanche Rego

14

A cup of chai halfway through the first Open House of the year is just what I need before I face yet another set of parents. Especially because the rain is lashing at the windows and there's a strong breeze.

Most of my colleagues hate parent-teacher meetings, but I don't. Perhaps because it's just my second year of teaching and my first at this school, I'm gung-ho about every aspect of school life. Yes, it's demanding—but so is everything worthwhile in life. PTMs, in my opinion, are the vital link between school and home—yikes, I sound like a B.Ed. textbook!

Usually, parents only ask how their children's marks can be increased, as though there's a magic switch that is going to do the trick. It's tiring to give the same spiel, parent after parent. As a good teacher, you try your best to glean something about their home, and their backgrounds that can help you support their child better. And as my colleagues and I often discuss, parents of children doing well at school make regular appearances at PTMs, and those whose parents you really need to see rarely make it.

Another knock on the classroom door. It creaks open. There's Adi. The tall, thin woman must be his mother.

'Welcome, Mrs Krishnan, please do take a seat,' I begin with a smile.

'Please call me Delna. I'm so glad to meet you at last. Adi loves your classes, to say the least.' Her bony hand meets mine in a firm handshake.

Adi looks down; his mother and I smile. She signs the attendance register.

'Thank you, Delna. It's my pleasure to have Adi in the class. It must be your excellent upbringing—Adi's such an out-of-the-box thinker blessed with a prodigious vocabulary! I've displayed some of the students' artwork—Adi's work is up there on the wall.'

We both look at Adi who gives us a half-smile.

'How is he doing? All well?'

Delna slides on to the bench, leaning towards me. Thanks to her slim frame, she can sit comfortably on the students' bench.

'Please take a look at his marks.'

I push the marksheet towards her, she barely glances at it.

'That's fine, I've seen his papers. I have no complaint whatsoever regarding his performance,' she pauses. 'Adi, why don't you wait outside?'

Adi leaves the room rather reluctantly.

'Miss Blanche, I hope you know something of Adi's background.'

Rarely do parents broach sensitive topics themselves; I'm all ears. 'I know you are a single parent. Must be tough.'

'That's not what I meant. Yes, I'm divorced but everything's hunky-dory, to say the least. In fact, last month, Adi and his sister spent a weekend with my ex-husband's family. No problem there, I assure you,' she says.

She proceeds to tell me about his disorder and the psychiatrist's recommendations. It comes to me as a shock. Mrs Roberts had warned me of children whose names spelled trouble. One of them was Adi, but she had given me no further details.

Notwithstanding an academic understanding of ASD, I had no prior experience of managing such children. In Adi's case, he was a high achiever, which made things better in some ways and more difficult in others, I'm sure.

'Miss Blanche, thank you for your attention, it's the first time that I've felt heard in this school.' Letting out a long sigh, Delna continues, 'If Adi misbehaves, would you please let me know before it gets blown up into something big as it happened earlier? Needless to say, I hope this stays between us. His classmates shouldn't catch a whiff of his condition. Children can be mean sometimes—'

'No worries. My lips are sealed, Delna.'

'Thanks, Miss Blanche, I really appreciate your support. And thanks for seating him with the new student, Suzila. He feels quite responsible about helping her. As you know, he really doesn't have any friends at school or anywhere else, for that matter. I am hoping this may help to open him up to his peer group.'

I'm so glad Suzila's name has come up. I've been wondering what to do about Suzila. She seems to have some learning difficulties, maybe she can consult Adi's doctor? Delna readily agrees to my suggestion.

'Would you like to talk to his doctor, Miss Blanche?'

I don't see the need to at present, but I take the phone number to be passed on to Suzila's mother.

I thank her and assure her that I will do my best for Adi.

She slides out of the bench effortlessly, we shake hands, she moves towards the door and turns back.

'Oh shoot, I almost forgot! Adi's keen to get a part in the Christmas play. I know he's not much of an actor, but perhaps a bitty part could boost his confidence? I don't want to push it, but if you could please try, Miss Blanche? I don't want to take any names, but year after year, the same students are chosen for these events.'

The words rush out of her mouth, the creases on her face deepen. I simply nod. I don't want to promise her anything because I've already seen the list of names for the Christmas event, and Adi's name doesn't figure there.

Delna walks towards the door, apologising for taking up so much of my time.

There's another knock, and the door opens slightly. It is Mohit, followed by his parents.

Seeing the exchange of icy stares between Delna and Mohit's parents convinces me that therein lies a story to be investigated further. Sometimes I feel less like a teacher and more like a detective!

Mohit's parents spend a short time as they are only interested in ways to push up his marks.

Delna D. Krishnan

15

And at last, it's New Year's Day!

After a quick morning visit to the agiary and a lunch of last night's leftovers, we've been cooking, cooking, cooking, for our evening feast. I miss Suryamani big time!

Adi offered to help but Mummy was ~~ferocious~~ adamant about not having him in the kitchen. He helped with laying out the table.

It's been raining all day, hope our guests don't drop out. They trickle in slowly and by 7 p.m., everyone's arrived—Sujata, effervescent as usual, Sid, Vibs and Sreekumar. Sreekumar's in his trademark khadi kurta; poor guy, he's being sized up by three pairs of inquisitive eyes!

Mummy insisted on buying us new clothes. I feel a tad overdressed in a raw silk strawberry fusion outfit from FabIndia, but never mind, it's a celebration. Jas is looking cute in an orange-blue jumpsuit bought from some mall and Adi's in formal black trousers with a white shirt. Mummy herself chooses to wear one of her heirloom saris—pale green with a Parsi-embroidered border. We rarely see her in a sari, so it's quite a treat.

Sujata and Sreekumar are firstly fascinated by the rangoli patterns done by Jasmine and Adi at the entrance of the flat, then by the oil lamp at the altar with pictures of my dad, grandparents, aunts, uncles and other ancestors.

'Please tell us, aunty—isn't muktad like *shraddh* for us Hindus?' says Sujata, turning to Mummy.

'I'm not too sure what shraddh is, but muktad is the period when we offer our prayers for the departed, for the onward journey of their souls. Ten days of the choicest food and drink, ten days of prayer, ten days of mourning, ten days of bliss,' Mummy explains.

'Well said!' says Sreekumar, pushing his spectacles up.

'A period of mourning, yes. A period of bliss? Both are not possible at the same time,' says Adi, knitting his eyebrows.

'Mummy is right, Adi. It's a period of mourning because our forefathers are no longer alive, but the joy comes from our faith that they have come to visit us,' I butt in before the conversation gets hijacked by Adi's quips.

'And every day we make dishes that Grandpa used to like,' says Jasmine, linking hands with Vibha. 'Prawn kebabs were his favourite, so we made them three or four times, didn't we, Mamaiji?'

Mummy nods.

'Kebabs happen to be your favourite, as well, Jas,' laughs Sid, pointing his finger at her. 'Very convenient!'

'I take after my grandpa, don't I, Mamaiji?' retorts Jas cheekily.

We all join in the laughter.

'More than eating, it's about the prayers in the agiary and at home. Gives me a lot of peace,' says Mummy. She pours out the lemonade and passes the platters of paneer tikka around the room.

'We don't observe a ten-day period, but All Souls' Day is our version of the same thing,' adds Sid.

Mummy gives him an approving nod. If she could, she'd get Jas married to Sid here and now. She doesn't realize Sid and Jas are kids; and this attraction will most likely fizzle out. I'd certainly be happy if it lasts, but we'll cross that bridge when we come to it.

The kids disappear into Mummy's bedroom from where we hear peals of mirth and music from time to time. The adults continue talking about various customs. Adi remains with us, raptly attentive.

Mummy's carved rosewood table is weighed down with delicacies, painstakingly prepared: egg salad, chicken cutlets, mutton biryani, *patra ni machhi*. I didn't want the hassle of cooking today, but Mummy was adamant that our guests should have nothing less than homemade food. I know that her knees are giving trouble, but I didn't want to have a row about it, so here we are. Sid's mother has sent us an almond sponge cake, so we order some vanilla ice cream to go with it.

The conversation sparkles like Mummy's crystalware as the food is polished off. At some point, Sree asks the children about their hobbies. Adi launches into his pet subject—snakes—and everyone is amazed at his knowledge. Adi's taken aback by Sree's ability to match his knowledge. The glint in his eye indicates that he's about to throw him a curveball.

'Do you know what's a DBWS?'

'A diamondback water snake, am I right?'

Adi doesn't give up. 'A DBWS is nonvenomous but often confused with the venomous cottonmouth. Do you know how to differentiate between the two?'

'That I don't. You tell us, Adi.'

'The DBWS has vertical lines on the upper jaw and close-set eyes, giving it a goofy appearance. Cottonmouths have hooded eyes on the sides of their heads without the vertical upper jaw lines.'

'Your passion for the subject is phenomenal, Adi. Very impressive.' Sree reaches over the table to shake hands with Adi.

The slight smile on Adi's face indicates his elation.

'All I know about snakes is that Cleopatra was bitten to death by an asp,' says Sujata.

'Perhaps,' says our scholar. 'An asp is an Egyptian cobra. I read that after the defeat of her army, she killed herself either with a desert-horned viper or some kind of poison, such as a lethal cocktail of hemlock, wolfsbane and opium.'

'Can we talk of something else now? All this talk of serpents and poison on an auspicious day doesn't augur well,' says Mummy.

Everybody agrees, especially Sujata.

'Have you been to any forest area in Mumbai, Adi?' asks Sree.

'None of us have, Sree,' I say.

'Forest in Mumbai's concrete jungle? Never heard of such a thing,' Mummy sniggers.

'There are a few pockets. Why don't we go since Adi's a naturalist?' says Sree.

All of us, except Mummy and Sujata, agree.

'How about some singing, Jasmine? Your mom raves about your voice,' says Sujata, winking at me.

Jas jumps to her feet, pulling Vibha up with her, and both of them do a rendition of Meghan Trainor's 'Title'. Not to be left behind, we shout out the line, 'Give me that title, title', until Mummy restrains us. We must be creating quite a nuisance for our neighbours, she says. Thank goodness Naju's away dining at a five-star restaurant, courtesy her deep-pocketed son-in-law, otherwise, she'd be the one to complain first thing tomorrow morning. It's almost midnight when our guests leave.

Long after the guests are gone, we are still parked on Mummy's four-poster bed, exhausted but laughing and singing as we discuss the evening. Mummy and I finish off what's left of the wine, and the kids lick up the last of the dessert. The evening has gone exceedingly well, Sree gelled beautifully with the kids. ~~Perhaps we can think of a future together?~~

Adi Krishnan

16

Assembly spills over into the first period. Such a shame. My favourite bio period. Gone for a toss.

Kananbala, Mrs Roberts and the Grade X teacher are on stage. He glowers and lectures us. A Grade X student splashed the wall in the second-floor girls' restroom with the F-word. Why is the whole secondary section being admonished ?

Suzila's sniffling next to me. I offer my handkerchief. I don't want my shirt to be stained by her phlegm or tears. She says she's very scared. I tell her to stop crying. We haven't done anything wrong.

'You're such a good friend,' she whispers. She deposits some sticky stuff on my forearm as she leans over. 'Why didn't you come to Ankita's birthday party? Everyone was there except Shakeel, who had Covid, and you.'

I wasn't invited. None of my classmates include me in any event. Not that I care.

Suzila's quite touchy-feely these days. At the singing competition audition yesterday, she sang, 'You Can Count on Me Like One Two Three'. She was looking straight at me. I want to put an end to this nonsense. I'm supposed to help with her studies. I really like the sandwiches—sometimes chicken, sometimes ham—her mother packs. But that's it.

The first period bell goes. We are freed. Sweaty, jostling lines of students move up the staircase, muttering the F-word and a dozen others.

Miss Blanche meets us at the door of our classroom. 'I want to return your journals, students. Adi, can you get them from the staff room, please, and distribute them when you can?'

In the staffroom, teachers are guffawing about something. They take no notice of me at the door.

'Nothing new; this is a yearly occurrence,' says Miss D'Souza.

'That's why fees are increased every year, not our salaries. Desks and benches need repairs; walls have to be painted over,' Mr Prasad sniggers.

'Very shameful. But what else do you expect from today's generation?' says Mrs Varma. She sees me at the door. 'What are you doing here, Adi? Shouldn't you be in class?'

She waves me in when I explain. They fall silent. I collect the journals and leave quietly.

Walking back, I spy Mrs Roberts. Slithering into our class. Like an African twig snake. Spells trouble.

When I go in, every student is sitting ramrod straight. Mrs Roberts is in deep conversation with Mohit at the teacher's desk. She pats him on the back and sends him back to his seat.

She turns to the class. 'I have come to announce the names of the students for the Christmas play.'

I can't believe my ears! It's only September, and the actors for the Christmas play have already been finalized.

This year. I will perform. In the Christmas play.

She reads them out. Don't hear my name.

'Can you please repeat them?' I ask.

She reads the list a second time. There's Mohit, Riya as expected, and a few others. Suzila's name is completely unexpected.

'You haven't read my name yet,' I protest.

The class titters.

'I can't read your name if it's not on the list, Adi,' says Mrs Roberts. She peers at me over her glasses. 'Those whose names are listed will meet me after school. Practice begins next Monday.'

'On what basis are these names selected?'

'I won't tolerate that impertinent tone, Adi. Your English teacher has made the selection based on the poetry recitation test,' hisses Mrs Roberts.

Mrs Roberts leaves. The class flings words like 'weirdo' and 'freak' around.

Shakeel says, 'Armadillo thinks he's Tom Cruise.'

Mohit replies, 'Of course he is, didn't you know? Tom Cruise of the ant world.'

The whole class is in an uproar.

I throw my compass box at Mohit. It misses him narrowly. I take careful aim with my water bottle, but Suzila snatches it from my hands. Mohit's acolytes restrain him.

'Shut up! Why are you hounding him, guys?' Suzila stalks towards Mohit like a bullfighter.

The class quietens.

'If it means so much to you, take my part. I'll tell Mrs Rao,' Suzila adds, sotto voce, but they catch her words.

'Be careful, guys. Armadillo's got a bodyguard who's ready to take on the world for him,' says Andy.

More titters follow. I'm ready for a fistfight, Dr Parekh be damned.

Mr Prasad arrives. His bellowing voice silences everyone. He begins to dictate Hindi notes for the upcoming exams. That's all he ever does.

In the break, Suzila disappears. I was hoping to eat her sandwiches. Although Mom says I shouldn't eat hers daily. I eat my idli chutney.

The bell rings. The maths teacher comes and barks out instructions for the next set of problems. Only then does Suzila come back.

We work furiously for both periods because the teacher never wastes a minute. Her pace suits me. The rest of the class hates it. Someone says, 'Bad smell', pointing at Ronnie, the usual suspect. The teacher pays no attention.

The next class is a free. The history teacher is absent. The substitute teacher takes the class to the playground. She allows me to go to the library to research snakes.

Miss Blanche makes a surprise entry in the last period. She's exchanged classes with the Marathi teacher. She begins with a PowerPoint presentation, then moves to the blackboard, drawing the Venus flytrap. Everyone pays attention in her class. Why? She's passionate about her subject. Respectful to everyone. Even the nasty ones.

All of a sudden, Suzila shrieks. Somebody's chopped off an inch or two of both her pigtails. I'm part of the howling racket without meaning to be. Because I can't stop myself. She looks kind of pathetic.

Miss Blanche blasts us. She says, put yourselves in Suzila's shoes and reflect on the cruelty of this action. I don't have pigtails, so I can't imagine. I join the others in hanging my face down.

We are asked to write down our feelings. The one responsible is supposed to include a confession. I write a paragraph about how girls can protect their pigtails.

The papers are dropped into a box. Miss Blanche reads each hurriedly. No one has owned up, she says.

Ankita suggests that every student's bag should be checked for scissors. Miss Blanche pokes her nose into each school bag. Five scissors are unearthed before she reaches our bench.

In my bag, she finds not only scissors but also clumps of hair.

'These scissors are not mine, miss! I haven't done this, I swear.' I get to my feet. My eyes bounce from hers to Suzila's.

Suzila clamps her hand over mine. 'I know you couldn't do such a thing, Adi. It's a mean trick being played on you and me!'

Miss Blanche believes her. She collects the evidence from my bag and says, 'I will get to the bottom of this, students, even if it takes time. This kind of behaviour is appalling.'

The bell for dispersal goes. We mumble end-of-day prayers. We queue up to go to the school bus.

17

Sujata and I have a free period together, and wonder of wonders, the staff room is devoid of other human beings! After three back-to-back classes on a Monday morning, I'm more than ready for a relaxed chit-chat over a cup of chai, however over-sweet and lukewarm the tea may be. Kicking off my sandals, I settle down on the chair next to her with my cuppa.

'So how was your Sunday outing? Did you take in any of the mangroves or were you just Sreekumar-gazing, huh?'

'Stop ribbing! You know it wasn't just him and me, we were quite a large group.'

'C'mon, Delna, end the suspense, out with the details. I want to hear everything!'

'Sujata, the Vikhroli mangroves are incredible. Hundreds of acres of private forest. Did you know the forest stores six lakh tonnes of carbon? It has more than fifteen mangrove species and thirteen crab species...'

'*Woh sab theek hai.* Tell me, did you and Sree grab some private moments?'

'It was absolutely fascinating. Sree was able to share plenty of information, we spotted an otter and a mongoose, and the kids were so excited! Of course, Adi was both excited and afraid but kept hanging on to me and asking Sree if he could point out any snakes. Thanks to Suzila, he climbed up to the observation spot for a bird's-eye view of the extensive area.'

'Who's Suzila?'

'Adi's new classmate. At last, my son has a friend! She's from Nagaland. The girl has reading and writing difficulties, although she's bright. In fact, her mother got in touch with me. Dr Parekh ordered some tests that showed she's quite severely dyslexic. Her mother burst out crying seeing the results. I had to counsel her that dyslexia can be managed well. And remind her that Suzila is blessed with so many talents—singing, dancing, sports, art. Can't blame the mother entirely for her reaction. She's also a single parent, and sometimes it can be rough, needless to say!'

'Divorced, eh?'

'No, her husband has passed away. She works as a hairdresser during the day and a hostess at a Chinese restaurant in the evenings. They are living at a cousin's place till she can afford to rent a flat.'

'I see. How about Sid? Was he there?'

'Oh yes, Jas and he kept disappearing to click selfies. And god knows what else they were up to! He's a sweet kid, very well brought up, but lately Jas has been giving me a hard time, Sujata.'

'The classic mother-daughter syndrome! Don't forget, she's a GenZ.' Sujata gives me one of her knowing looks.

'Generation A, B or Z doesn't matter, but I'm struggling, Sujju. At first, it was insistence on going overnight to a farmhouse in Lonavala to bring in Vibha's birthday. I had to put my foot down—I'm quite tolerant, but going out of town to a house full of youngsters, with booze flowing freely spooked me out. While she lives under my roof, she needs to respect the house rules. What say, Sujju?'

'Makes sense, Del.'

'Then, the college is organizing a trip to Sri Lanka, and she was pleading with me to let her go. Sid and her gang are all going.'

'That should be okay, no?'

'Yes, but I can't afford it, Sujata. She wanted to ask Krish for the money. Mummy thinks that's fine, but I don't want to seem like a beggar. I promised her next year—one of my fixed deposits will mature, so a trip should be doable.'

'Poor girl!'

'And she's hell-bent on getting herself tattooed. She's sulking right now. Only talks when required. Yesterday's outing thawed things between us. Let's hope it lasts.'

All is quiet for a while except for the whirr of the ancient fan that does nothing to dissipate the deadly combo of heat plus humidity.

'How did you bring up three girls, Sujata? Please give me some lessons!'

'I've had my fair share of trouble, believe you me! Even though my daughters are now settled in their careers, and have their own families, with every new crisis, they come running to me!'

'Being a parent is a thankless and unending job, as my mother often says!'

'This too shall pass, Delna. That's my guiding philosophy,' Sujata wraps her arm around my shoulders. 'Don't be too hard on her. She's a sweet kid.'

'I know she's a sweet kid but exasperating too. And now the landlady wants a fifteen per cent increase in rent, or we'll be kicked out. House hunting and moving, gosh, I really don't need this right now!'

'That's a shame, Delna. But you will deal with it.'

'When I shared this news with Mummy, she brought up moving in with her once again. And you know, that would be disastrous.'

'C'mon Del, let's drown your sorrows in another cup of canteen chai.'

As she returns with two cups of chai, the admin assistant enters the staff room and informs Sujata that she is wanted in the principal's office. Gulping down the tea and grabbing her books, she moves to the door.

She turns theatrically to face me. 'Delna, you have avoided mentioning anything about Sree and you! And I'm not going to let you off so easily.'

'What do you want me to say? Yes, it felt good having him with my kids. Cosy and comforting, if you know what I mean, but—'

'Let's leave out the *but* for now! Catch you later.' With another of her winks, Sujata vanishes.

I really know less and less what my own feelings are! And what's going to happen on multiple fronts in the near future.

MOHIT BANSIWAL

18

I've perfected the art of avoiding the CCTV cameras in our lobby by pulling my golf cap low and by slinking in and out of the lift on the seventeenth floor, then taking the stairs to the eighteenth. Not for nothing is 'Move it like Mohit' a byword in school.

WTF. One lift is closed for maintenance work, and the other has been broken since yesterday. Taking the steps two at a time, I pause for a sec at the tenth floor. Who else but nosy Naina flings her door wide open.

'*Jai shri* Krishna, Mohit. *Kem chhe*, beta? Mummy-pappa *maja ma*? Haven't seen your mother for days. She didn't show up for the kitty either.'

'Jai shri Krishna, aunty. Mummy's gone for the *char dham yatra* with her sisters.'

'*Su vaat chhe*, beta. Your mother sets an example for all of us. Pappa must be working very hard, no? And your brother?'

'Papa's busy as usual. Dheeraj bhai is in Sangli, at the engineering college.'

'*Aavje*, beta. I'm only a phone call away if you need anything.'

Like hell. Even if I were dying, she's the last person I'd think of calling for help. She's the ultimate WhatsApp queen of Eternity Towers, skilled at spreading rumours and gossip. Once I heard her refer to Dheeraj and me as '*bade baap ke bigde hue bete*' and here she's dripping milk and honey. As though I'd be so easily fooled. Papa came from an insignificant village in Rajasthan and made it big on his own. What is it to her if we flaunt our wealth?

I'm able to get into my flat without any more interruptions. It's a pit stop before heading to Shakeel's for the night. His parents are away at their Karjat farmhouse, so it is the perfect time for us to get together.

Shit, voices in the living room. Papa and a female voice? Isn't he supposed to be away on a business trip? Better to announce my arrival before they set eyes on me.

'Hello, Papa. It's me.'

There is a pause. Then he speaks in an unusually hearty voice. 'How nice, Mohit. Come, beta.'

Something fishy going on. As I enter, I see I couldn't be more right. The female's trying to smooth her skirt with one hand and her hair with the other while the top button on her shirt remains undone. Papa's frequent work trips and Mummy's remonstrations had sown suspicions about Papa's *extracurricular activities*, but this is the first evidence. Got to hand it to him, he seems to be handling the situation like a pro.

'What a surprise! Weren't you supposed to be at your friend's place? This is my colleague, Nayantara.'

He laughs nervously, sounding more horse than human. The female waves at me with a slight smile.

'And don't tell your mother. We're having chicken lollipops with a small drink before we get down to work.'

My eyes were still checking out the female. Papa's words divert my eyes to the coffee table, to the bottle of Black Label, the ice cubes and the lollies. Mummy doesn't mind liquor too much, but she would be totally freaked out to see any non-veg food entering her holy citadel.

I smile back.

This totally ruins my plans. I was here to grab some booze and the keys to his new BMW, but Papa's on his own trip. Neither looks possible. Got to think of something real quick.

No harm trying, at least for our weather-beaten Honda. I started driving at the age of twelve, in our gated complex at first. Now I ferry Mummy to and from the temple, the restaurant, and the beauty parlour, as long as these places lie in the bylanes; can't get caught on the main road or the highway. Both Mummy and Papa are super proud of my driving prowess.

'Papa, do you need the car or are you going to be working at home? I'm going to Shakeel's and wondered if I could—'

'Yes, yes. Shakeel's the one who lives in the next lane, eh?'

I nod.

'Nayantara, my son is a superb driver. What reflexes! He didn't need driving lessons, just picked it up naturally.'

'What else can we expect? He's your son, sir.' The female flashes a toothy smile.

'Not only driving, but good at studies and sports. Even my older fellow. I have no complaints, so why stop them from having fun, eh? Young blood, after all.' He pauses, to take another sip. 'And Nayantara here, she's very hard working, Mohit.'

The female blushes.

'I'm sure she is, Papa.'

'Take the car. Drive carefully, beta. You can never tell when these careless pedestrians appear in front of your vehicle and always, always it's the motorist at fault. Here, keep this cash handy. In case you run into the police.'

He just wants to get me out of the house! He hands me about five thousand rupees, with another nod.

I'm out, jiggling the car keys. Thankfully, the lift is back in operation.

What about the booze now? Let me text Dheeraj bhai to order it for us. Bhai sends me a thumbs up with some choice *gaalis*. Deed is done. I'm on my way to celebrate with Shakeel and his building friends.

With the music system blasting heavy rock, my mood's on the upswing. Bring it on, ACDC, Led Zeppelin, Guns N' Roses . . .

The enthusiastic reception by the guys loosens me up further. This is turning out to be a good evening after all.

'*Kya haal hai*, Mohito? Eagerly waiting to hear about your shenanigans, especially the strange-but-true tales of Adi manav!' says Mohsin, poking me in the ribs.

'Give me a break, guys! I get enough of freaky-deaky Adi at school.' My smile says it all. 'But yes, he's one-of-a-kind.'

'Wait till you hear this, guys. In the short break yesterday, Adi manav was talking to the crow that came to our classroom window. He insisted that it's the same crow that mimics Prasad Sir in the Hindi class. When Andy made fun of him, the weirdo chased him with his WMDs,' says Shakeel.

'WMDs?' asks Jatin.

'Sharpened pencils, bro, nothing much else, but he refers to them as Weapons of Mass Destruction,' Shakeel clarifies. 'Mohit and I have often been at the receiving end of those weapons.'

'IFOs too!' I add.

'What are IFOs?' Mohsin asks.

'Identifiable Flying Objects like water bottles and compass boxes that are flung out at anyone within striking distance.'

We all collapse to the floor with laughter.

'A guy like that belongs to a mental institute, doesn't he?' says Jatin.

'Not quite. School would be dull without guys like him. Must say he's been less violent in the last couple of months. Don't you agree, Shakes?' I say.

Shakeel nods.

'His report card must have nothing but zeros!' says Mohsin, slapping me hard.

'He's an all-A student, bro. That's the funny thing. When he talks, it's like he is stupid, but when he writes, he makes a lot of sense.' It's something I've never figured out. Another thing I've never figured out is why he readily shares his notes and ideas with others, even me, his arch-enemy.

Sometimes, I pity the guy. It must be so terrible to be a loser like him; stumbling, mumbling, fumbling. Speaking, loudly and awkwardly. You ask him a question, and he repeats the question back at you. And at the same time, he just does not seem to realize what a loser he is. He seems perfectly happy, most of the time. And then it annoys me that I waste my emotions on him, of all people.

'Mohit's absolutely right. There's always a race among Mohit, Riya and Adi for the top spot, guys,' says Shakeel.

'Heard of crazy cool but never crazy clever,' Mohsin laughs.

'Talking of Riya, what's the latest, Mohito?' Jatin asks.

All four look at me expectantly.

'Yeah, yeah, tell us. Have you touched base, bro, or do you need lessons from us?' Mohsin eggs him on.

Meanwhile, the doorbell announces the arrival of our much-awaited alcohol and stops their line of enquiry. Our glasses get filled and refilled until the haze of well-being hovering over our heads settles deep down in the pit of our bellies. Adi and Riya and everything of daily interest fade into the background. The Spotify playlist blares our faves. Life couldn't get better.

At some point, Jatin picks up the thread of conversation again.

'C'mon, bro, what are you and Riya up to these days?'

'Riya's too prim and proper, and Mohit's kind of done with her. He's got the hots for the new girl, Suzi, don't you, my monstrous Mohito?' Shakeel's trying to speak even though his tongue's gone heavy.

'Nah, bro, Riya, I've known her since I was a kid. Almost feels like a sister to me now. And her arms are like a wrestler's, have you noticed, my dear Shakes?'

'Never went near Riya coz she's your gal, but now that she isn't, I'll check out her arms and more. Thanks for the heads up, Mohito!'

Shakeel pours out another round of drinks. All three of them clink their glasses, 'To Riya!'

'Who's this Suzi babe? Tell us more, Mohito!'

'Suzi's interesting but too fragile and childlike. It's Rosie who's my flavour of the month!'

All four of us link our arms and raise a toast. 'To Rosie!'

'Rosie, of all people? Why, Mohito, why?' asks Shakeel.

'Under that shapeless school uniform, she's quite something.'

'How do you know?' asks Shakeel.

'Her insta reels are very revealing, bros. Pun intended—revealing!' I add.

'This babe seems worth checking out. Can I become her follower too?' asks Mohsin.

'The more the merrier. Once she sees you as my friend, she'll confirm your request, not to worry.'

Mohsin and I hug. Jatin disappears to the bathroom, either to throw up or to pee, or both.

Shakeel's tandoori fish and prawns stay untouched, No one can coordinate their limbs enough to serve themselves. One by one, the guys pass out on the floor.

I'm the last one standing—got to put off the music system, stick the food in the fridge and rest awhile.

Suzila Sangma

19

I'm thirteen today! Never before have I celebrated my birthday at school, never before have I had friends over for my birthday, never before have I felt so nervous.

They'll be here very soon. Mama thinks it's a good idea, let's hope so.

I'm wearing make-up for the first time, glitter in my hair, and three-inch heels. I'll be able to look eye-to-eye with Riya, at least.

The school day went very well. Miss Blanche made my birthday super-duper special! She asked all my classmates to come up to the front of the class one by one and say, 'Happy birthday, Suzila! You are special because . . .' And everyone complimented me about something or the other—my dancing, singing, artwork, and agility. There were a couple of snide remarks about my eyes and small frame, but I ignored them in the glow of the others.

The best was from Adi, of course. He simply said, 'I like her sandwiches.'

The entire class cackled. Miss Blanche said, 'Anything else, Adi?'

After a pause, he said, 'You are special because you are my friend.'

So sweet, na? He lends me his notes, explains concepts patiently and treats me better than anyone I've ever come across. The class thinks he's crazy; I think he's super innocent and earnest.

I didn't invite the whole class, how could I? Our flat is not so big, it's not even our flat. Neither can Mama afford to host the party at a restaurant. Just Mohit, Riya, Ankita, Shakeel and Adi, along with his sister, Jasmine. I wish I had an elder sister like Jasmine to look out for me . . .

Adi and Jasmine are the first to arrive. Adi brings me a drawing of a coral snake, with its red-yellow-black hues, because he knows I like bright colours. Jasmine hands me a box of chocolates. While we wait for the others to arrive, Jas and I warm up with a few Elvis numbers. Mama accompanies us on the guitar.

The others come. Jasmine begins shimmying, asking us all to dance. Everybody, except Adi, readily starts twisting and jiving. Mama keeps the guitar strumming.

Mohit says, 'C'mon, Adi manav. Time to loosen up!'

Jasmine pulls Adi into the circle. He shuffles uncomfortably for a bit, then goes out to the balcony.

Flushed and tired, we fall to the floor laughing, teasing and generally having a good time.

'I'm dying of thirst, Suzila! Can we have something to drink?' says Shakeel.

'Of course, not just drink. Let's cut the cake and have some snacks,' says Mama.

Adi returns to the room and asks, 'Are we having chicken sandwiches, aunty?'

'Hope not,' says Riya, scrunching her face. 'I'm a vegetarian, aunty.'

'Maybe bats and snakes, Suzila?' Mohit snickers.

'Snakes, especially for Adi!' Shakeel slaps Mohit on the back.

'Guys, let's see what aunty has for us,' says Jasmine.

'Everything is vegetarian, not to worry!' Mama smiles and disappears into the kitchen, with Jasmine trailing her.

Jasmine brings out the red velvet cake to 'oohs' and 'aahs' from the gang. This kind of cake costs the earth, but Mama got it at a fifty per cent discount from the restaurant where she works. Mama follows her with cold drinks and snacks.

'Momos? Wow, I love them!' gushes Ankita.

'I know, Suzila told me. Momos and hakka noodles, made at home!' says my ever-smiling Mama.

'It all smells delicious, aunty! Guys, let's get on with the cake cutting. Don't know about you peeps, but I wanna attack the goodies here,' goes Jasmine, lighting a candle.

There's a single marzipan rose on the cake above the message, 'Welcome to the teens!'

'You're a baby, Suzila! I turned thirteen last year!' giggles Riya.

'Man, I must be a dinosaur! Seventeen going on eighteen,' chuckles Jasmine.

After the birthday song is sung and I've cut the cake and I've shared a bite with Mama, the girls pick me up and give me thirteen plus one birthday bumps. Shakeel crushes the rose and smears it all over my face before I can back off, with Riya and Ankita pinning my arms down.

'That's mean. Dirty. Disgusting, Shakeel. She looks like a clown now!' says Adi, seething with anger.

I wipe it off with a tissue as best as I can.

Mohit opens his mouth to deliver a stinker, but Mama cuts him off. 'Never mind, Adi. Everything's allowed on a birthday, right? C'mon, my teenaged wonder, go wash up and bring back your pretty face.' She hands out the plates and starts serving the snacks while I run into the bathroom.

When I return, everyone is busy eating. Mohit and Shakeel are discussing their favourite shows. Riya and Ankita are cribbing about studies and teachers. Mama is sharing the momo recipe with Jasmine. Adi looks bored.

'Do you have any books to read, Suzila?'

I hate reading but I had a couple of books that were given to me by my aunt, so we go into the bedroom to look for them. They are far back in the cupboard behind my schoolbooks. I hope I can find them.

'Is this your dad?'

Oh no, Adi has noticed our family pictures. I wish I hadn't brought him in, but it's too late now.

'Yeah.'

'He's dead, right?'

I nod. If only Adi would shut up.

'When did he die?'

'Last year.'

'Was it a heart attack?'

I nod because I can't let him know the truth: my dad was a good-for-nothing alcoholic and drug addict. Mama and I guard this terrible secret from everyone. That was the reason that brought us to Mumbai— Mama wanted to make a fresh start.

'My dad is alive. He doesn't stay with us. Because they are divorced. But he's a great guy. Next time he comes here, you can meet him.'

Tears are stinging my eyes, and I turn my face away. My dad was a horrible man. I never wanted anyone to meet him ever. Mama used to feel sorry for him, but I never did. She said it's a sickness, but I can't forgive him.

'Hey, Adi, let's head home now. I wanna work on my project,' says Jasmine, poking her head in.

'Okay. Bye, Suzila.' Adi gets up and turns his back on me.

Wiping away the tears, I go out into the living room. Everyone's ready to leave. They thank Mama and make their way out.

'Aren't you glad we invited your friends? Wasn't it a nice evening, my precious girl?' Mama pulls me into her arms and kisses me. 'Will you help me wash up and put things away before Uncle Lipichem arrives?'

I follow her to the kitchen silently.

The evening was great and yet . . . How can I tell her how difficult it is to pretend that my dad died of natural causes? My classmates are so lucky living their happy lives, never worrying about money or fathers who haunt you from beyond the grave.

Jasmine Krishnan

20

Honestly, I didn't wanna go with Mom, but when it's for Adi, I feel as protective of him as she does.

Mom and I are facing away from each other, looking out of the rickshaw impatiently. The traffic is crawling, not even a semblance of a breeze. The sweat running down my face is just what I need for my acne, man.

These days, the only thing that keeps me sane is Zeba. Every evening, the frisky little pup and I go for a walk round the block. Zeba wants to stop at every pole and sniff at every human or non-human thing by the road; her poop has to be collected and yet, Zeba makes my day. She's loving, she's loyal, she's non-judgmental—that's my Zeba. She can't bark like a fully-grown dog, so she yelps in an inimitable Zeba fashion. The moistness of her nose, her tongue that licks my face—I could go on and on about her virtues.

I want her to sleep in my bed a couple of nights a week. H&M won't mind, but my brother says an absolute 'no' to that.

My phone pings. Sid is out shopping, and wants my input about a jacket he's going to buy. Brown is not his colour; I text him to go for the navy blue or olive green. Sid can't take any decision on his own these days, but what's gonna happen next year? He's gonna pursue architecture and I'm gonna . . . Who the hell knows what I'm gonna study? That means we won't see each other daily. Life's not fair at all!

At last, the traffic begins to move. Our rickshaw driver manoeuvres the vehicle any which way to get us to our destination.

A huge crane is blocking the entrance to the school. Oh yeah, Adi's been telling me about the deafening racket from the building work next door. And he can't stand loud noises. My baby brother must be going insane.

The admin assistant acknowledges our presence after fifteen minutes of waiting in the lobby.

'Sorry, Mrs Krishnan, Dr Jose had to leave for a sudden meeting with the education inspector. But Mrs Roberts will see you shortly.'

Five minutes later, Mrs Roberts comes towards us, grinning sheepishly. Adi's right, she does look like an African twig snake.

'A very good afternoon to both of you! Let's sit in the principal's office.'

She leads us to Kananbala's den, then instructs the canteen over the intercom to send three glasses of water when we decline her offer of tea.

'So nice to see you, Jasmine—always a pleasure to see our ex-students. How are you, my girl?'

I give her a curt smile. Mom had warned me not to be over-friendly.

'Mrs Roberts, I'm going to get straight to the point,' says Mom.

Mrs Roberts nods.

'You know I never come to school with a complaint. I'm aware I have a child with special needs. He may display some socially unacceptable behaviours even though the intent is never wrong. But this time I'm not going to stay quiet.'

Mrs Roberts nods once more; her tongue keeps darting in and out, wetting her lips.

'This episode was beyond the limit of anything that can be considered acceptable!'

'Adi was badly hurt, I understand.' Mrs Roberts offers a placatory smile at Mom, who disregards it completely.

'Let me refresh your memory, Mrs Roberts. The day before yesterday morning, when Adi was in the school bus, there were unexpected showers. The strong winds blew some rain into Adi's face, and he got up to shut the window. The bus braked, he was propelled forward and he accidentally stepped on Mohit's toes. In return, Mohit punched him. The bus nanny informed you about this.

'Regardless, Dr Jose summoned Adi to his office and asked him for an explanation. Mohit was not called to the office, let alone reprimanded for his deliberate act of violence. When my son returned home the day before, he had a black eye and a sprained wrist. And that evening, I was ejected from the class WhatsApp group.

'Thanks to Suzila's mom, I got wind of their evil motives. They wanted to petition the school to expel Adi for his violent ways! They talked about my being a frustrated single mother who's a bad influence on Adi!'

The housekeeping staffer brings in a tray with glasses of ice-cold water. Mom's remains untouched, but both Mrs Roberts and I knock ours back.

'At the beginning of the academic year, my child was suspended even though it was his classmates who played a trick on him. Now it's almost the end of the first term and again he's in trouble. What is going on here, Mrs Roberts? What would you do if he were your child?'

'Calm down, Mrs Krishnan. At first, we didn't know what had happened. Now we have investigated—'

'Exactly what I mean! Before knowing the facts, you assumed that anything that goes wrong must be Adi's fault! There seems to be one set of rules for my son and another for the rest of the class.'

Mom coughs, refuses the glass offered by Ms Roberts, and continues. 'The next day, his bio journal was discovered in the trash can! Why is my son being victimized? When I texted Mohit's mom, she ignored my message. I called her, and she disconnected my call. Would you call this civilized behaviour?'

'According to the rules, you are not supposed to get in touch with a parent and take matters into your hands, Mrs Krishnan. However, we have spoken to Mohit's parents.'

'Just *spoken*? No punishment for him? I've also come to know that Mohit's family is related to the trustees. Does that explain why he's receiving special treatment?' Her eyes blazing, Mom finally pauses to take a sip of water.

'Nothing like that, Mrs Krishnan. They are all children. At their age, mischief is natural, but we are trying our best to discipline them.'

Mom ignores her words and reaches into her bag. She fishes out the letter that she had dictated to me to type for her, last night. The letter is so well drafted, it sounds like a legal document, man. 'Here's a letter that I've written to the principal.'

'No need for a letter, Mrs Krishnan.'

'I absolutely insist. This letter must stay on record. If you don't take this seriously, I'll be forced to go to social media, and who knows what will happen then.'

Now Mrs Robert's shitting bricks. She gulps down Mom's glass of water and accepts the letter reluctantly. Her smile is growing weaker by the minute.

'We have had a long relationship, Mrs Roberts, from the time Jasmine was in school. We will take the necessary action, I assure you.'

Mrs Roberts' eyes swing like a pendulum from me to Mom and Mom to me. She looks kinda pleading and her voice comes out like a squeak. 'Yes, take my word. You can send Adi to school from Monday. Hope Adi is feeling better now. Will you have some tea, please?'

'It's too hot to drink tea. Now this other thing. What a pandemonium! Can't you get the construction work to happen during non-school hours? Adi can't tolerate loud noises because of his condition. Every day he comes home with a headache.'

'We have complained to the BMC. These things take time, Mrs Krishnan. In our country, you know how it is.' Mrs Roberts smiles slightly.

Mom gets up and sails out like a battleship, with me following her like a little lifeboat.

As soon as we are out of the gate, she says, 'Mrs Roberts is so stuck up—not a word of apology.' She wipes the perspiration off her face. 'Come Jas, let's have some ice cream before heading home. I need something to cool down.'

In that moment, I feel nothing but admiration for her strength, her chutzpah, and her love for Adi that will make her stop at nothing. Man, my mom, she's Wonder Woman.

Shirin Ardeshir Daruwala

21

All of a sudden, Delna has changed her tune. Mark my words, nothing will come out of all this.

So far it was 'Adi must stay in this school, come hell or high water', and now it is 'he deserves a better school.' So much so that Krish flew down to Mumbai, and the two of them visited four or five schools together. Mark my words, Adi will give her pain wherever he goes because that's part of his DNA.

Last night, Delna and I had a hush-hush dinner with Krish at his hotel where we scanned the schools they had visited, discussing the pros and cons of each. The fees are more or less the same, but cost isn't really an issue as Krish is ready to pay the fees. Eventually, we zeroed in on one that seemed to be the most suitable for Adi.

Delna went home and broke the news to Adi. He didn't take it well, but he's not too pleased with his present school, so he's not that opposed to the idea. Dhoor ne dhefar, if he were my son, I'd just spank him and say, 'This is what your dad and I have decided', and that's the end of the discussion. But my opinion is not called for; I'm just the grandma who is expected to fill in when required, like this morning.

Darling Delna had a paper presentation at Mumbai University, so Mamaiji accompanies Krish and Adi to the chosen international school. Off the highway, along a nondescript lane, a right turn on to a short driveway leads us to the imposing U-shaped building. It is more like a five-star hotel than a school, with marble pillars and huge ugly chandeliers, centrally air-conditioned, the cool air smelling lavender fresh. The front desk receptionist, wearing enough perfume for us all, greets us in the foyer in dulcet tones. Her American accent is as carefully cultivated as her gelled blue-and-silver nails. Smartly turned-out housekeeping staff, fluent in English, appear with mineral water, followed by tea and coffee in bone-china mugs, sugar cubes in crystal bowls and almond biscuits. Soft western classical music streams out of well-concealed speakers. We sit on plush faux leather sofas, glass-topped teapoys placed strategically between each sofa set in the high-ceilinged foyer.

Delna had asked me to dress well, as though I need advice in that department, especially from her! Here I am in my coral pink pantsuit, offset by a white handbag with my white pumps, grey hair neatly brushed, and pearl drops in my ears. Suited-booted Krish is pacing up and down nervously, on the phone, managing his work in Singapore. Adi, seated next to me, is absolutely quiet. Soon he's whisked away for his admission test by a teacher with a gentle, pleasing manner.

Krish requests the receptionist for a school tour for my benefit, as he and Delna had already seen the facilities. We are escorted to a hallway boasting six elevators. The elevator moves noiselessly to the mezzanine floor, where we are shown the Olympic-sized swimming pool, indoor basketball court, the cafeteria, the music studio and the auditorium. We get a view of the ample grounds with dedicated areas for cricket, baseball and soccer. In the auditorium, we view a ten-minute audio visual about the school philosophy and achievements.

'How do you like it, Mrs Daruwala?' Krish asks me when we return to the foyer.

'What is there not to like? I wish I could study here as well! The infrastructure is mind-blowing!'

'The teachers are very well-trained too. There's a resource room for children with special needs, you know. We met the principal yesterday, an experienced educator from Australia.'

'Perfect. I see one problem, though. Will he be able to fit in with these children of *dhapdhapiyas*?'

'I didn't get you? Dhapdhap . . . Mrs Daruwala?'

'Sorry, it's a common expression. I mean, rich people. Students who can afford this kind of fees must be coming from wealthy homes. They will be driving up in fancy SUVs. Our Adi will be in an autorickshaw or at the most, in my tiny little Maruti Alto.'

'I see what you mean. If you ask me, a school like this will surely take care of socio-economic differences. Let's hope he performs well in the admission test.'

'Adi will do well in the test. No problem there.'

I pat Krish on the back. At last, he's getting involved in his children's lives. Geetha is a good influence on him, mark my words.

'Let's be positive, I say. Besides, it's close to the house, very convenient from every angle.'

'Yes, provided they continue to live there. Hasn't Delna told you yet? Their rent is being pushed up quite a bit, so she may have to vacate this flat.'

'She hasn't breathed a word of it to me!' Krish looks at me with fire in his eyes.

'You know how she is, Krish. She doesn't mean it badly; she's just too proud to burden others with her troubles.'

His brow furrows and his voice rises. 'Do I classify as *others*? We may be divorced, but her welfare is and will always remain my concern. Why would I come here to find a school for Adi if I didn't care?'

'I know and appreciate all that you are doing, Krish. So does Delna.'

'I don't think Delna has ever appreciated anything I've done for her! If she had, who knows? We may still have been married,' he shrugs. 'Sorry, I shouldn't be saying these things to you. She's your daughter, after all. Don't get me wrong, I admire her. She's trying to do her best for the children.'

'Krish, she may be my daughter, but I'm not blind to her flaws—she's headstrong to a fault! Please don't say that I've shared this house thing with you. She'll get mad at me!'

We smile at each other conspiratorially.

'Rest assured, I won't. But tell me, has she found alternate accommodation? Don't you see it's vital before we freeze on the new school? How can she be so irresponsible?'

What else can I do but nod my assent? He resumes pacing up and down. Adi returns, shoulders slightly drooping.

'How was your test?' both of us ask Adi.

'Test over. Nothing much. Ready for home.'

'What does that mean, son?' Poor Krish, foaming at the mouth, grabs Adi by his shoulders.

'Very easy, Dad.'

'Are you sure?'

'Yes.'

The pleasant teacher comes back to inform us that the results will be emailed in a week's time.

The friendly security guards wish us a great day ahead as we move out of the school, and back to the heat and dust of Mumbai.

'Dad, I want you to meet Suzila. Will you come home this evening?'

'Wish I could, Adi. But my flight leaves tonight, and I have a meeting at the bank now, so we'll do it next time, okay?'

Adi nods.

Delna's rejoicing; Adi has a friend now. Dhoor ne dhefar. Agreed Suzila's a sweet girl, but certainly not like regular kids. She's also got a mental problem, and she's always asking for his help. Mark my words, this friendship won't go very far. And if it does, it will bring its own set of woes.

Blanche Rego

22

The staff room is unusually quiet. All heads down, correcting the midterm papers. I'm fighting sleep; marking piles of papers is no joke. After the euphoria of reading the first few wears off, every answer begins to look the same. And you really have to look keenly for subtle differences so that your marking is fair. Even students who sleep through class are more than alert when it comes to marks, ready to fight for an increase of even half a mark.

What's disturbing is that Adi's grades have fallen, perhaps for the first time. Adi's been so withdrawn, totally unlike himself, this whole month. On the other hand, Suzila has done marginally better.

His eyes devoid of repentance, Mohit had handed Adi a letter of apology the day he returned to school. The detective in me wants to find out what makes Mohit behave in this manner. I don't believe that children are mean or revengeful without reason, but my colleagues warn me to keep away from Mohit because of his family's ties with the school management. I do want to reach out to the goodness in Mohit's heart, but it may be better to bide my time. I don't want to lose this job.

I've tried to engage Adi in conversation, but his responses have not gone beyond 'yes' and 'no'. Besides the fistfight with Mohit, he's cut up about not getting a part in the Christmas play, but is that all there is to it?

When I spoke to his mom, I came to know that he has been offered a place in an international school. They haven't taken admission yet, as they would like Adi to complete the school year. Adi's fretting and fuming about this big change. Delna appealed for my help in finding out what is going on in his mind.

I could do with a little break. It's PE period, so Adi will most definitely be in the library. I put away the papers in my locker, do a few neck and back stretches and walk towards the library.

As soon as I push open the door of the library, the musty smell of old books hits me. Whenever I mention to Mrs Roberts that we need to rejuvenate the library, she grumbles about the lack of funds. I'm positive that we can take the help of the PTA to raise funds or ask parents to donate books they no longer need or do something else. The bottom line is that we need to have books that children will be interested in reading. Our conversation always ends with Mrs Roberts telling me, 'You worry about your subject, let the librarian and the English teachers take care of this.'

There he is—nose in a book—as expected.

'Hello, Adi. What are you reading?'

'Good morning, miss. It's called *Uncover Cobra*.'

'Interesting?'

'Very. Do you know what happens when one king cobra bites another, miss?'

'Nothing happens. Because it's immune to venom of its own kind. Am I right, Adi?'

'Yes, miss. How did you know that?'

'I guess it has something to do with my being a biology teacher, Adi!'

Thank god, he's in a chatty mood. I must broach the topic of the new school.

'Is snitching on your friends good, miss?' The question comes abruptly.

'I suppose not, Adi. On second thought, it depends on the context.'

Wonder what he's getting at . . .

'What is more important—loyalty or honesty, miss?'

'You are asking me some really tough questions, Adi. Both loyalty and honesty are equally important, according to me.'

'But what is more important, miss?'

'I really can't answer that unless I know what you are talking about.'

The book is slammed shut. He gets up and starts pacing up and down, hands stuffed in his pockets.

'Is there something you would like me to know, Adi? Did something happen in our class?'

He stops pacing and looks straight into my eyes. This is most unusual for him. 'Will there be consequences if I tell you?'

'Why don't you sit down, Adi? Let's hear what it's about before I respond.'

'You know Suzila is my friend, miss.'

I nod my head, though he is gazing at a bookshelf nearby.

After a pause, he continues, 'She copied my answers in the exams, miss. She said we are friends, so it's fine.'

'And what do you think, Adi?'

'It's wrong. It's dishonest. It's unfair. But I don't want her to know I told you. And I don't want her to be punished, miss. And please, don't tell Mrs Roberts.'

No teacher training course prepares you for something like this.

'I see. Thanks for your trust in me, Adi. Let me think about it.'

How could anyone not love this kid? All the other teachers judge Adi for thinking too much of himself. Mr Prasad, the Hindi teacher, referred to him as a *badtameez* in the staff meeting.

When Mr Prasad had scolded Adi once, the kid had looked down without saying a word for a couple of minutes. Mr Prasad had demanded an apology. Adi had said, 'Don't disturb me. I'm trying my best to control my anger.'

Mr Prasad had been appalled by this disrespect towards authority, and everyone else in the staffroom concurred. I thought it was an honest answer.

None of the teachers seem to take Adi's condition into account. Are they even aware of it? The same goes for our principal. Dr Jose is a good man, but too old-school for my liking. He seems to be only interested in appeasing the education department and obtaining good results in the board exams.

'There's something else, miss.'

I don't know if I can handle any more today.

'Riya chopped off Suzila's hair.'

'Really? How do you know, Adi?'

'Riya confessed to Suzila.'

'Really? What was the reason?'

'Riya was jealous of Suzila. Because Mohit was paying her attention. Now Mohit is paying attention to Rosie. Riya and Suzila have become good friends. Because of the Christmas play.'

'That means Suzila must be real mad at Riya!'

'No, miss. Now they are best friends. Suzila has forgiven her.'

Everyone in the school knew about Mohit and Riya being a couple. But this other stuff, how come I've missed seeing it?

'I hate keeping secrets. I feel burdened. Don't tell anyone, miss.'

'I can't promise anything, but I shall keep it between us for now, Adi.'

At least he doesn't reject my words. Now I've found a bargaining chip. 'Adi, there's something I wanted to talk about.'

I pause so that I can get his full attention. 'Your mom told me about the new school being considered for next year!'

'Nothing is decided. We may be moving to another house.'

'Yes, I heard that too, but isn't the new school business exciting? Hearty congratulations! You did excellently in the admission test, I heard.'

His shoulders droop, and his jaw clenches. He looks to his right and left, although there's no one but him and me, barring the librarian and her assistant in a far corner.

'I don't want to leave. How can I go there? Without you? Without Suzila?'

'Sweet of you to say this, Adi. I'll miss you, too. But the new school has very good teachers and small class sizes. I'm sure you'll be far happier . . .'

'There's no guarantee, miss.'

The kid is so right; he's wise beyond his years.

'Nothing in life is guaranteed, Adi, but we must be open to new adventures. Promise me that you'll think about it.'

'Okay, miss.'

I leave the kid alone. He has given me so much to think about, I doubt I can go back to marking papers.

Suryamani Kumar

23

Tough day, daily chores done, curtains washed and ironed, bedsheets changed, and now I'm shelling the beans for making *titori* in a coconut sauce. Tedious, very tedious, but aunty likes to eat sprouts, and this one is her favourite.

I still have plenty to do—set the yoghurt for tomorrow and fix an evening snack for Adi and Jasmine. Adi is cycling in the compound, and Jasmine is walking Zeba. When they return, they'll both be like ravenous foxes. I want to finish everything *jaldi-jaldi* to catch the 5 p.m. serial.

The doorbell is ringing as though the fire brigade is here! Must be Jasmine. Why has she come back early? She's always so impatient! One of these days the bell will go *phut* and we'll have to call the electrician to replace it. Aunty will grumble about more expenses.

'Suryamani, you won't believe what happened!' squeals Jasmine.

My eyes pop out. Zeba is in Adi's arms, she's licking his face and he's not protesting one bit! Jasmine is hugging her brother.

'What happened?'

'Adi was taking rounds on his bike, and I was nearing the gate by the lane. Sid called so I stood near the gate while Zeba sniffed around—you know I don't talk on the phone when I'm out on the road. I don't know how and when my grip on the leash loosened and Zeba ran out into the lane—'

'Baba re baba! Did Zeba get hurt or something?'

'Adi spotted Zeba in the path of a van backing into our gate. He threw his bike to the ground, ran across, picked up Zeba and brought her back to me, without a single scratch! No cap, my baby brother, you are the best!' She kisses him on both cheeks.

'What else could I have done? If Zeba had been crushed, Mom would have been furious. And H&M—who knows—they may have sued us,' says Adi, finally putting Zeba on the floor.

'*Shubh shubh bolo*, Adi. Thank god, nothing went wrong!' I bend down to pat little Zeba. 'Naughty girl, Zeba, why did you run on to the road? You never do that when you are with me.'

Tiny Zeba keeps circling Adi's feet, yapping in happy bursts.

'I'm famished. But first, I must shower. Zeba's saliva is all over my body!'

'Me too, very hungry. What's the snack today, Suryamani? And please take Zeba back to her house. We've had enough excitement for the day.'

There goes my serial. Let me get rid of Zeba before she sheds any more hair in our living room.

'Can you manage with a peanut butter sandwich? I still have to shell the beans for dinner, and I'm running late,' I ask at the door. Our flat keys as well as Zeba's are always around my neck, so I'm not locked out of either flat.

'We love peanut butter!' say Adi and Jasmine in unison, before disappearing into their bedroom.

Chalo, that's a quick-fix snack for me.

The doorbell again. Aunty's come, looking stressed.

'Suryamani, I have a splitting headache. Please make me a big cup of tea and get my pills. No auto at the college gate. And the buses, with people spilling out of them, were just whizzing by! I had to walk half a kilometre before finding an auto!!'

Aunty throws herself on the sofa, kicks off her sandals, stretches her legs out, and grumbles about how uncomfortable the sofa is.

'Sure, aunty.'

I make the tea *phat-a-phat*, get a glass of water with the pills.

Jasmine comes out with the phone glued to her ear. It vanishes into her pocket upon seeing her mother.

'Mom, I'm going to say sorry even before you start yelling at me. I did something wrong; I get it, but what Adi did was incredible!'

She tells aunty the whole story. In the meantime, I bring out the sandwiches, Adi's almond milk and Jasmine's cold coffee.

'Really?' Aunty smiles widely, looking relaxed. 'This is real good news! Dr Parekh did say having a pet is therapeutic for children like Adi. If Adi continues to bond with Zeba, he'll be less uptight. Even though what you did was irresponsible, Jasmine, I'm really pleased with the end result. Do me a favour, Jas—call Dad and tell him.'

Jas calls and shares the story with her father. Aunty gestures to Jasmine that she wants to add a word or two.

'Hello Krish,' she says. 'A real surprise, isn't it? Adi used to refuse to touch Zeba, let alone allow her to lick him or anything. And here he went out to save her! Remember, he's also scared of traffic, but this didn't stop him. People say children with ASD cannot display empathetic behaviour but you tell me, if this is not empathy, what is? This could well be a turning point for him, who knows?'

She looks very happy about the response from the other end. Next, she calls Mamaiji and gives her the news.

Adi returns, looking as red as a tomato. He must have scrubbed himself so hard trying to erase Zeba's licks.

'*Maro dikro*,' goes aunty. 'I'm so proud of you, my *jaan*. You did something very brave.'

Adi gives her a half-smile. 'It's all because of Jas. She's so careless, Mom.'

'You are one hundred per cent right, Adi. Let's see, her weekly allowance will have to be withdrawn for a month,' says aunty.

'Okay, Mom, I'm ready for the consequences. And I'll never do this again. I promise. But . . . can we keep quiet about this incident, or do we have to tell the truth to H&M? They may forbid me from ever taking Zeba for a stroll. And that would be unfair, wouldn't it?' Jasmine looks worried.

'How are you even asking, Jas? The truth, however uncomfortable, has to be owned up. You know that; it's something both Dad and I have drummed into your heads from the time you were little.'

'Even if we don't, the security guards or anyone else who was down will surely inform H&M as soon as they enter the gate,' says Adi.

Aunty laughs and that helps everyone relax.

I go back to shelling the beans. Jasmine lends a hand. We put on FM radio and sing along, softly at first, then at the top of our voices. Soon, dinner is ready.

Why should I lie? TV soaps are not half as interesting as the drama in our household.

Suzila Sangma

24

It's PE period. Because Ankita is down with typhoid, I'm substituting as captain of Red House. This means I will be leading the march past for my house on Sports Day, which is coming up soon, too. We are on the ground; I should be at my happiest, but I'm dragging my feet.

Miss Blanche confronted me during the lunch break about my cheating in the exams. She didn't raise her voice, agreeing to keep it between us if I promised not to repeat it in the future.

How could she have known—it had to be Adi who told her. I thought he was my friend. Nobody can be trusted in this world, I swear.

Adi comes towards me when the teacher calls for a loo break. His excuse didn't work today. He had to be down for marching practice as all students from all four houses have to participate in the march past.

'Andy is giving me a hard time,' he says. 'I wish I were in your house. You wouldn't shout at me if I couldn't march in sync. You know coordination is my problem.'

'How can you blame Andy? He's doing his job as captain of Blue House. Even I would do the same. The teacher has given us captains this responsibility.' I spit the words out without looking at him at all, my shoe tracing knots and crosses in the dirt.

'Really? I took you for a friend, Suzila!'

'And so did I, Adi!' I make an about turn and march away.

'Have you broken up with Adi?' Riya runs up beside me. She must have overheard our conversation.

'As though Adi's my boyfriend!'

'C'mon, Suzila, the whole class knows the two of you are kinda cosy.'

'Then you are mistaken, Riya! You are my buddy; I wish you wouldn't talk like that!'

I jog away from her towards the boundary wall until the teacher calls us back to resume practice. Enormous amounts of the dirt from the construction next door has made its way to the playground. When will the school get it cleared?

I take my position at the head of the Red House, waiting for the signal to commence the march past. Students are looking bored and fagged out. One hour of PE at 2 p.m. is no one's idea of fun. Even though October has slid into November, the heat is unrelenting.

Adi's right ahead of me. His spot is in the last row of Blue House, at the far end where he won't be visible to the audience on Sports Day. That's where all the laggards are placed.

'It's broiling hot. The wicked wind besides. Throwing up an awful lot of dust. I can't stand it!' He coughs and splutters, but no one takes any notice of him.

When the practice is over, Mrs Roberts announces that Red House has given the best performance and makes a special mention of me.

The gong for dispersal sends hundreds of feet kicking up dust like a herd of cattle. We make our way towards the school building.

Riya sidles up to me, congratulates me, and whispers, 'Hey, I didn't mean to upset you. Friends?'

When I stretch my arm to give her a side hug, my sour-smelling armpit comes in the way, so I give her a high five instead.

Adi must be right behind me because I can hear him coughing and sneezing.

Someone yells, 'rats', and all hell breaks loose. Everyone runs in all four directions, despite the teacher's repeated whistles prompting us to stay in line. More and more dust is kicked up.

Riya and I zigzag our way through the hordes of students and make it inside the building. All the restrooms are overflowing with students splashing water over themselves and each other. Serpentine queues at the water fountains. Eventually, we get back to the classroom, but there's no teacher. Shakeel cracks a joke about the rat in the playground.

'That wasn't a rat! That was a bandicoot! Didn't you see how big he was?' says Adi in between sneezes.

'And Adi, don't you know bandicoots are found only in Australia?' says Riya, looking over her shoulder at Adi, and at the same time, squeezing my arm.

'That's a marsupial. Not to be confused with the Greater Indian bandicoot. This is part of the rodent family on the Indian subcontinent,' says Adi.

'*Achha baba, tu* Shivaji,' says Riya. 'I'm really not interested in increasing my GK, least of all on the rat family. As it is, my brains are fried today.'

We all laugh some more.

'If there are rats, there are bound to be snakes as well,' Adi shouts.

'Snakes in the heart of Mumbai. Isn't that an exaggeration, Adi, even by your standards?' says Shakeel.

'Not an exaggeration, Shakeel! They may come to meet our snake charmer here!' laughs Andy.

Andy and Shakeel start doing the cobra dance. Other students join in.

'I don't care what you think. Don't come running to me if you see a snake!' Adi shrieks.

The loudspeaker crackles. The principal's voice comes on.

'Students, please listen carefully. We have received an urgent circular from the Mumbai police.

They have cautioned us about the movement of drug dealers near schools and colleges in Mumbai. On the pretext of selling candy, they lure students to their stalls and turn them into addicts. For your safety, please do not approach these vendors. Strict action will be taken against students who disobey these rules.'

There's a slight hush after this announcement, then everyone starts talking all at once, discussing whether they have seen or heard of these vendors near our school.

Andy says, 'Quiet, class, I've got a brainwave. Let's ask Suzila if she's come across a drug vendor.'

The class quietens. All the faces turn towards me.

'Why Suzila?' Riya asks.

'Drug addiction is common in Nagaland, your state, isn't it?' he asks.

I nod.

'That doesn't mean she knows anything about it. Mumbai has the highest reported drug abuse cases in India,' says Adi.

'Stop giving gyan, wise guy. Suzila knows all about it from personal experience. Her father died of a drug overdose,' says Andy.

My face goes white, my hands are clammy, and I don't know where to look. How did Andy find out?

'Her father had a heart attack. Didn't he, Suzila?' asks Adi.

The tears come fast and furious. I shake my head. My world is crumbling. We thought we had escaped my dad's sins, but there's just no way out and nowhere to hide.

'That means you lied to me. On your birthday—' asks Adi.

'That's quite enough, children,' says Miss Blanche, who seems to have appeared from thin air. 'Drug dependency is an illness, and we are sorry for what happened to Suzila's father. But that does not mean we're going to make Suzila feel bad or gossip about it. No one is going to mention this ever again. Do you hear me? Come here, my girl.'

She takes me by the hand and steers me out of the classroom.

I crumple in her arms and sob into her shoulder. 'How did he find out, miss?'

'I don't know, dear girl. But it doesn't matter. I won't allow them to broach this topic with you. If they try, let me know immediately,' she says, her arms protective around me.

Delna D. Krishnan

25

When will this ~~torture~~ ordeal end? What a lousy way to spend my Diwali vacation. Two more flats seen and rejected. The broker makes every deal look attractive, but when you see the apartment, something or the other will be wrong with it: too small, too dilapidated, too unsafe, too far. Or, if the apartment is fine, the rent or the deposit will be too high.

I have already informed our landlady that I will be vacating her flat by 3 December. The clock is ticking. I have less than a month to find a new flat. If push comes to shove, we can move in with Mummy temporarily, but that won't be the ideal solution.

Krish is really disturbing my peace. Now he is stressed out about Adi's new school. Some friend of his has children who study there, and Krish heard of a Grade XII student's suicide. The case is being hushed up, but there seems to be a connection to drugs. There's a heavy drug and alcohol scene among its high school students, he says. I think this is common to all schools in Mumbai, but Krish is very worked up.

Also, he's pushing his 'Dad card' for Jasmine's tattoo. Geetha got one when she was thirteen, and so it is fine for Jasmine to get one too. Jasmine already had Mamaiji's support, and now Dad's as well. ~~I'm the only villain here.~~ How long can I fight it?

It's six in the evening, but the sky is already dark, the monsoon has finally retreated. It's less humid these days, which also means the pollution will rise. Covid and other viral diseases will make a comeback. Hardly anyone wears a mask. I must insist that the children keep up the habit.

'Mom, why does the emerald tree boa have two spurs at the base of its tail?' Adi appears with his snake book just when I need some peace and quiet.

'Adi, can you leave me alone for a while, please? Today's was a really unsuccessful house hunting trip. I can't be bothered about anything, however fascinating it may be.'

'Mom, Jasmine and I don't want to move to a new place. Why can't you take Dad's help? Then we can continue to live here.'

'We've talked about this, Adi. You know that I'm not going to take anyone's help. Please do not irritate me.'

'Okay. I'm going down with Zeba.'

Adi shuts the door with a bang, and I smile! I'm so glad about his newfound love for Zeba. When Jasmine decided to spend a week at Mamaiji's place, Adi volunteered to take Zeba for a round every evening. Initially, Suryamani had to accompany him because he refused to gather the poop, but now he wears a mask and gloves and scoops up the poop. Zeba and Adi have grown closer, and he doesn't even feel unclean when the pup licks him. He takes Zeba to their bedroom and reads to her from the snake book. Zeba barks in between to show her understanding, I guess. Dr Parekh was right; he does seem calmer these days.

The bell rings. Suryamani must be back with the groceries. No, it's Mummy and Jasmine! How come? She's not supposed to be back until the weekend.

'This is a surprise! What's up?'

'I can't seem to handle either of your children. Ask Jasmine what happened.'

Jasmine just runs to their room and shuts the door! Now what?

Mummy sits on the sofa, and I slide to the floor.

'What happened, Mummy?'

'I don't know. Since this morning, her eyes have been puffy and red. She keeps going to the bathroom and throwing up. She's listless, no appetite, won't talk to me.'

'Must be indigestion. Did you order some takeout? Chinese doesn't agree with her sometimes.'

'Dhoor ne dhefar, we've been eating home food. I make whatever she likes. Everything was fine until today. When a young girl throws up, what is the first thing that comes to one's mind?'

For a moment, I'm nonplussed, then the penny drops. 'Mummy, what are you trying to say?' I stare at her in shock.

No response.

'Oh shoot! You can't be serious?' I pause. Mummy holds my stare. 'Don't tell me, you said this to her!'

'Of course, I did.'

'How could you? No wonder she's upset!'

Meanwhile, Suryamani's returned home.

'Suryamani, go knock on the door and ask Jasmine to come out. Then make some strong tea for all of us.'

Suryamani calls out to Jasmine and raps on the bedroom door several times. No response.

'Mummy, she must be totally freaked out, to say the least. This isn't a 1950s Hindi movie that you can accuse her of being pregnant. I doubt it very much, but even if she is, it's not the end of the world.'

'Sorry, Delna, I don't subscribe to your liberated ideas. Better for all of us that I return home and leave you to sort out your own mess.'

Mummy tries getting up from the sofa but falls back.

'I agree with you, she's too young, Mummy, but you're being melodramatic. I'm sure there's a perfectly good reason for her nausea. Let's find out.'

The phone pings. It's Krish. I'm not in the mood to talk to him, so I ignore the call.

I get up and rap on Jasmine's door. 'Come out, sweetie; it's all right. I'm sorry if you are offended. You know Mamaiji; she doesn't mean anything bad.'

Slowly, the door opens and she comes straight into my arms, sobbing.

'My little munchkin, shall I give you something that will help to settle your nausea?'

She starts coughing and sputtering and runs back to her bathroom. I follow her and rub her back while she keeps up the crying and vomiting. Bright green and yellow stuff makes its way out. The smell makes me want to puke as well, but I take deep breaths and hold it in.

'What did you eat, jaan? You seem to have some bug. Let's call the doctor, okay?'

I call out to Suryamani to stand beside her while I get my phone. No answer, I leave a message for the doctor. It's Krish, again.

'Krish, I'm busy. I'll call you back . . . WHAT?'

I see the reel he's sent me. Now I need a doctor or at least a glass of water before I pass out. What's wrong with Jas? How could she do this? What's wrong with my upbringing that she could succumb to these cheap thrills?

The doorbell rings. Mummy opens the door. Adi's back.

'Mamaiji, where's Jas?'

Before she can respond, I say, 'Adi, please wash your hands and get some water for Mamaiji and me. Make it quick.'

He does as he's told without any questions for once. Then he goes into their bedroom but returns in less than a minute.

'Mom, has Jas been bitten by a snake?'

Mummy snorts.

'Adi, please spare me your theories. Go, stay with her, and send Suryamani here.'

When Suryamani comes out, I ask her to squeeze lemon juice and sprinkle a little sugar on a few ice cubes.

I turn to Mummy and hand her the phone.

'Mummy, see this reel forwarded by Krish. Now you'll know what's wrong with Jasmine.'

Mummy's eyes grow bigger and bigger as she watches the reel. 'When did she do this? Is she out of her mind? I thought she's the sensible one here . . .'

'We'll ask the questions later. Now let's concentrate on helping her recover.'

'I still don't understand. How did Krish get this video?'

'The video's gone viral, Mummy! Geetha happened to see it and passed it on immediately.'

Mummy's at a loss for words. That's rare, of course.

I return to their bathroom. Finally, Jas has stopped puking, but she's pale and can barely walk. Adi and I help her to sit on her bed and she takes small sips of the drink prepared by Suryamani. I keep one arm wrapped around her until she falls asleep.

'Is she going to die, Mom?' asks Adi in all seriousness.

'No, she'll be fine by tomorrow at the latest, Adi.' I can't help but grab him and kiss him on his forehead. For the first time, he doesn't push me away; instead, his arms close around my back. I kiss him some more. We turn off the lights, draw the curtains and go into the living room.

Krish calls once more. I assure him that Jas is better. He wants to have a word with her, but I tell him to wait until tomorrow.

None of us have any desire to eat, so we have some more cups of tea and try to nap, leaving only one table lamp on in the living room.

After a couple of hours, Jasmine is up and looking much better. Mamaiji and Adi are sleeping. I think it's the best time to talk to her about what she did.

'I saw the video, Jas. What made you do this?' I ask, trying my best not to sound angry.

'You know?' She looks scared now.

I nod.

She narrates the whole incident. She had seen this trending challenge and thought it would be fun to acquire more followers. So, she made a reel of herself eating fifty green chillies. Vibha was supposed to join in, but chickened out at the last minute. Last night she had a slight burning in the stomach, but then it escalated through the night and by this morning she was miserable.

'I never thought it would go viral!' she says.

'I'm not so concerned about it going viral or not. I'm concerned about your taking on this challenge—

it's a form of self-harm, isn't it? Why would you do something like this?'

'YOLO, Mom. I didn't look at it as something dangerous, Mom. I'm sorry.'

She buries her head in my shoulder, and we stand with our arms around each other. I never want to let her go.

Mummy tiptoes out and wraps her arms around both of us.

'I'm sorry, Jasmine. I shouldn't have said what I did. You'll forgive me, no? Even adults can make mistakes, sometimes,' she whispers.

Jasmine doesn't say a word, but all three of us remain in a tight huddle for what seems like an eternity. Three generations of women who may get it wrong sometimes but who love each other madly.

Suzila Sangma

26

This is it. It's the annual Sports Day for the secondary section of the school. Five hundred children are on the school ground, watched by twice the number of parents.

The playground looks very different today. The seating area is covered by a red shamiana and the snacks area by a blue shamiana. Not much dust flying because the ground has been watered early in the morning. Even though it's the end of November, it's still hot. Today, I don't mind the heat. All I want is that Red House should win the march past trophy. Someday, I'd like to represent my state at the Republic Day parade in Delhi. And today is a stepping stone towards that dream.

Mama has arranged my hair into three braids with a white ribbon going through. My white-and-blue checked uniform is freshly starched and ironed and the brown shoes polished to a shine. I don't think there's a more smartly turned-out girl on the ground than me.

The school band drummer begins. I give it my best, calling out 'left, right' at the top of my voice. I can't see how the other houses are doing, I keep my eyes straight out front, only looking to my right when we pass the shamiana for the chief guest and other dignitaries.

The applause at the end of the march past is deafening. There are cries of 'Red House, well done!' and 'Hurrah for Blue House!' I don't hear any praise for Yellow or Green House. That means it's going to be either Red or Blue. Fingers crossed and heart in my mouth, please dear god, let the trophy go to Red House!

The races begin, and the chants grow louder. Teachers are waiting at the finish line with packs of glucose powder. Most people are rooting for the Class X students, a few for Mohit and Riya. I win the 100-metre race easily; not many strong contenders there. The longer races are not my cup of tea, but I'm going to be part of the relay.

We shout, we scream, and my voice grows hoarser as I cheer for Red House in every event. Overall, the Green House tally is climbing. The track events for the younger children carry on while we biggies move on to the field events. I glide through the air and land on my feet in the long jump event. Two medals earned—first place in the hundred metres and second place in the long jump. Mama will be so proud of me.

When I stand on the podium, I look for her but can't find her in the massive crowd. I hear Jasmine's clear voice cheering me—she's waving a red balloon for me! She's a sweetheart. So what if I'm not talking to Adi. She's still my friend.

After I run my leg of the relay and pass on the baton to Rosie, my ankle twists, and I collapse. Miss Blanche is called by the teacher on duty, and with her help, I hop towards the shamiana. At once, Mama and Adi's family rush towards me to check if I'm okay. They are all fussing over me, but I'm not willing to leave the ground. I want to hear the result of the march past competition.

Jas gets me a chilled bottle of mineral water.

'Where's Adi?' I ask. Got to be polite. I know he's not participating in any of the events.

'God knows. He was wandering on his own somewhere near the boundary wall when I saw him last,' says Jas.

I watch the events come to an end with my foot on Mama's lap. The whole school lines up for the results of the main events. I want to go as well but Miss Blanche says she and Jasmine will escort me to the podium in case my house wins.

Blue House clinches the march-past trophy. I'm disappointed but never mind, I've got my individual event medals. Mohit wins the overall best athlete award for boys. There's a roar of applause, as though he's won an Olympic medal. He's the darling of the school because of his looks and his attitude. Some boys hoist him up on their shoulders, and he poses for several photos and selfies.

There's a non-competitive tug-of-war at the very end. Some teachers and support staff also join in the fun. In spite of Mama's protests, I stand up on the chair to get a better view. If only I hadn't twisted my ankle, I would have been there.

With threats and counter-threats, the tug-of-war begins. Each side accuses the other of cheating and each time one side tumbles down, the other side crows and guffaws. Both sides are well-balanced, I think it's going to be a tie. Pushing and shoving, the teams come closer and closer to the audience. I climb on to a chair so that I get a clearer view.

Suddenly, piercing shrieks rend the air. There are some panicked screams of 'Cobra!' A cobra in Mumbai?

People at one end, near the wall, begin to scream and run away towards the school. More and more people panic and try to scurry at top speed. It would be funny if it were not so scary. No one seems to know what is happening. It seems a stampede is unfolding. Younger children are being knocked down in the rush. What's going on?

As that end of the field clears, I can see him. Mohit. His face is white, and his arms are flailing. As I watch, he lets out a blood-curdling cry.

Adi! That is *Adi* running towards him. I can't believe it. I have never seen Adi run.

Adi rushes at Mohit, and bends and picks up . . . a rope?

No! I can't believe my eyes! It's a snake!

Near me, Mrs Roberts faints. Some of the younger kids are crying. There is more screaming.

A real snake! He's holding it up in the air! The creature is trying to squirm out of his hands! Adi's movements are casual, as though he does this every day.

The gardener runs towards Adi and seizes the snake.

Jasmine and Delna Aunty race towards Adi.

Teachers and security guards try to control the situation. Dr Jose takes the mic and orders everyone to return to their seats, but it takes another ten minutes before order is restored.

Meanwhile, across the field, Adi is clearly lecturing the gardener. Mohit is throwing up in the nearby bushes.

Dr Jose goes towards Adi, as does Miss Blanche. They talk animatedly.

For the second time today, I can't believe my eyes! Dr Jose kisses Adi on the forehead! They come back to the shamiana area.

Dr Jose addresses us in his nasal voice. 'Parents, rest assured all the children are unharmed and a potential tragedy has been averted, thanks to our courageous student of Class IX A, Adi Krishnan. Without caring for his own safety, he saved the life not only of his classmate but everyone else on the ground.' He turns to cast another tender look at Adi.

'We thank you, Adi Krishnan, on behalf of the whole school. Jai Hind!'

Adi receives a standing ovation. The ground reverberates with the sound of 'Adi, Adi, Adi'. To my surprise, tears are streaming down my face as I link arms with Mama and Adi's mamaiji.

Mohit's parents rush to Adi's side and Mohit's mother folds him in an embrace! Adi looks dazed and tries to break free. Despite the excitement of the moment, I can't help but grin. Adi is always so exactly himself.

Mohit limps towards Adi and salutes him before embracing him. Adi, being Adi, looks deeply uncomfortable and then pushes him away.

The crowd applauds. Everyone's phone camera is in action. Many people want to shake hands with Adi, thump him on the back and take selfies but Jasmine and aunty form a protective barrier because really, everyone should know he hates to be touched.

Finally, the trio makes its slow way towards the stalls. I limp towards Adi. I've missed him all these weeks.

'Adi, you are the true champ today!' I pump his hand.

'Don't be overdramatic, Suzi. It was a rat snake. Completely harmless,' says Adi.

'How did you know that, my baby brother?' Jas reaches up to ruffle his hair.

'It must have been quite obvious to him, Jas. His knowledge about snakes is prodigious,' says Delna Aunty, beaming.

'In that split second to identify the type of snake and pick it up, it's very daring of you,' says Mamaiji, with pride in her eyes.

'Now can we go home? I need to wash my hands. So many people have touched me, yuck. Colonies of bacteria. Must be multiplying. By the minute. Let's hurry,' says Adi.

Jasmine Krishnan

27

Dad's coming to Mumbai for the day to attend a felicitation ceremony organized by Adi's school today. Adi doesn't even know—it's a surprise, man!

Mamaiji and I are pacing up and down the living room, waiting for Dad. Suryamani is assisting Mom with her hair. Except Mamaiji, we are all dressed in our Parsi New Year attire. Mamaiji is wearing an attractive peach-lemon pantsuit. Adi, sprawled on his bed, is engrossed in some or the other book.

We've kept the door open so that Adi won't hear the bell ring—aren't we clever? I hear the lift stop at our floor. Dad's aftershave wafts in before he does. He greets us warmly in his big, booming voice. I run into his arms and remain there for as long as I can.

Mamaiji makes a tremendous effort to get up from the sofa. Dad and I pull her to her feet together. She says, 'Welcome, Krish. I don't know how to thank you enough, Krish. You are by far the most decent man in the universe! May god bless you a thousandfold.'

Dad says, 'The pleasure is all mine, Mrs Daruwala. Does Jas know . . . about the other matter?'

Mamaiji winks at him. 'No one other than Geetha, you and I know about it.'

What are they talking about?

'Why are you here, Dad?' Adi's come out, followed by Mom.

'To see you all! Come here, kanna. I'm so proud of you.'

Dad thumps him on the back. Adi volunteers to give him half a hug. OMG, for my baby brother, that's a huge achievement.

'Dad, that happened two weeks ago. You congratulated me on the video call. Today we are going to school. There's a . . .' says Adi.

'Yes, yes, Adi, that's why Dad is here. He's coming to school for the felicitation. We wanted to surprise you.' Mom grins. I've never seen her smile so widely.

'Delna, you're looking great, I say,' thunders Dad.

Mom smiles warmly. 'Come, freshen up, Krish. Jas, please take Dad to the bathroom, and don't forget to give him a fresh towel.'

Dad and I chat as he washes up. After that, he examines the inside of my wrist.

'Let me admire your hard-earned tattoo, Jas,' he says.

'Thanks, Dad! You are the best. Without your support, Mom would never have allowed it.'

'Anytime, Jas. That's what dads are for!' He kisses my forehead.

'Dad, I want to tell you something very important.'

'Go ahead, Jas.'

'Dad, I've decided to become a chef. I'm gonna join a catering college. You're the first person I'm sharing this decision with. You okay with it?' I search his eyes for his approval.

He hesitates for a microsecond. 'Yes, Jas, yes! Whatever you want to pursue as a career, your mom and I will always support you. Your becoming a chef means I'll get to eat the choicest of food, made by my princess! What can be better than that?' He rubs his belly and winks at me. 'And your friend, Sid? He's going to be an architect? Are you still seeing each other?'

My head moves up and down vigorously. 'Next year, he's going abroad for college. I don't know if our relationship will work long distance. Sid says nothing will change, but honestly, I'm scared of the future.'

'I know, Jas. No one can predict the future, but whatever it is, your mom, your dad—we're always there for you. Please know that.'

Arms entwined, we return to the living room.

Dad booms, 'Adi, I want to know in detail about your snake act. Don't leave out anything.' He sits next to Adi.

Adi starts to narrate the incident, but none of us can keep quiet. We talk all at once, and each one of us adds our version of what happened that day.

Dad asks, 'Adi, tell me honestly: you weren't scared, even for a fraction of a second?'

'No. Some students were shouting, "cobra, cobra", but I knew at once that it wasn't a cobra at all. Rat snakes are much longer and have thinner necks.'

'But still, to pick him off the boy—what's his name—Mohit? The snake could have bitten you in self-defence.' Dad's face is full of admiration.

'It was a reflex action on my part, Dad. Mohit would have died of fright, so I had to get the snake off him, that's all.'

'Dhoor ne dhefar—Adi, you are being too modest! Mark my words, Krish, what your son did, was remarkable. It was quite the superhero act,' says Mamaiji.

Dad's belly expands with joy.

'But Dad, the snake story actually has a sad ending,' says Adi.

'Why? Was anyone bitten? The gardener?'

'No, Dad. The gardener killed the snake, instead of freeing him in the jungle or some such place.'

'I see what you mean, Adi,' says Dad.

'What could he have done in that moment, Adi? With so many children on the ground? Sometimes the ideal solution can't be found.' Mom sighs.

'And now, how are people treating you at school, Adi?' asks Dad.

'Nicely, Dad.'

'That's an understatement, Adi. Krish, both Mrs Roberts and Dr Jose apologised for the way Adi was bullied by his classmates and hounded by teachers. Now they have decided to appoint a school counsellor, and they have asked for Dr Parekh's help in formulating policies that will serve children with special needs,' Mom explains.

'The laughing stock of the school has had the last laugh,' I say.

'Nicely put, Jas,' says Dad.

'And what about his classmates? They treat him with respect now,' adds Mamaiji.

'I'm sure they'll get up to their tricks after this episode is forgotten, but their words don't rattle me as much as they used to,' says Adi.

'Very nice to hear all this,' Dad says. 'Adi, are you ready to join New Age International School?'

Adi shifts uncomfortably in his chair and looks at Mom. She doesn't say a word.

'Not really. If you insist, I'll do it,' says Adi.

Mom and Dad exchange a glance.

'Your mom and I have talked about it. If you don't want to, you can continue studying at this school. We realize that all schools have some good and some bad. It's a question of adapting to it, so the final call is yours,' says Dad.

'Okay, Dad,' says Adi in his mechanical voice.

I poke him in the ribs. 'Adi, did you hear what Dad said? You don't have to go to the new school! Yay!'

He says simply, 'Thanks, Mom and Dad.'

Mamaiji clears her throat. 'On that happy note, I want Krish to mention something very important. And please Delna, you will not react. Hear him out, I beg of you.'

What? What is happening here?

'Why don't you say it, Mrs D? That's better,' says Dad, looking down.

'Very well, if you insist. This is about your housing situation, Delna. Krish is willing to make the down payment on a flat. You have to manage the EMIs, Delna, for ten years, and then the flat will be yours. No more of this gypsy existence.'

'What are we talking about? What business do you have to decide on my behalf? Krish, I fail to understand you, to say the least! Shame on you, Mummy, for being a co-conspirator in this crazy scheme!' Mom mutters through her teeth, giving them her toughest look.

Dad pales.

Oh no! Are they going to have a row and ruin everything on this special day?

'Delna, calm down. Listen to me. It's Naju's flat, above mine. Naju is leaving—good riddance—to stay in some fancy tower, and her flat was up for sale. That's why Krish and I thought it's a god-sent opportunity! All you need to do is agree. Krish is ready to transfer the funds today,' says Mamaiji.

'Mrs D, let's not rush it. The decision is Delna's, no worries,' says Dad.

'Look, I didn't want to say it yet because the details are still being worked out, but I'm this close to finding us a new house,' says Mom, shifting uncomfortably in her chair.

'Really? Let's hear it then, Delna,' says Dad, looking at her.

'All of you, except Krish, know my friend Sujata. She's lived at her aunt's place in Chembur since her daughters moved out. She's now received a two-year fellowship at an American university, so the flat will be let out. I told her I'm interested, and her aunt, who lives in the US, is happy to rent it to a known person.' Mom smiles.

Honestly, Sujata's flat in Chembur?!

'Dhoor ne dhefar! You can't be serious about moving to Chembur?' says Mamaiji, disgust shining in her eyes.

'C'mon, Mummy, Chembur is not that far. Besides, I'll be getting it at the same rent as what I'm shelling out now,' says Mom fiercely.

'Rejecting Krish's generous offer and taking a flat on rent once again makes no sense to me, Delna.'

Mamaiji is not willing to give up. I must confess I would have preferred Naju's flat too, but I know Mom too well. She won't take any favours from Dad.

'Mrs D, if this is what Delna prefers, let's end this discussion here and now. I'm just glad that you have figured out something, Delna.' Dad shakes Mom's hand.

'Thanks, Krish. I appreciate the gesture.' Mom smiles some more.

'You can take it up on one condition, Delna,' says Mamaiji.

'And what is that, Mummy?' Mom's voice is getting frosty, man.

'You must agree to buy a new sofa set, Delna, before my back gives way,' says Mamaiji.

The house resounds with laughter, but Adi looks quite flustered.

'If we move to Chembur, how can I see Zeba every day?' asks Adi.

'Dhoor ne dhefar! Aren't you overdoing it, Adi?' Mamaiji shakes her finger at Adi.

'We can have our own dog, Mom, can't we?' I ask.

'We'll see,' says Mom. She keeps breaking into a smile.

'If we don't leave now, we'll miss the school function,' says Suryamani, emerging from the kitchen.

'Yes, everyone, get ready, go to the restroom, drink water, or whatever you need to do, we need to leave soonest,' says Mom, snapping her fingers.

Everyone says, 'Yes, Mom!', including Dad.

I bet you there isn't a happier fam than ours in the entire world today. No cap.

What is ASD?

Autism Spectrum Disorder (ASD) is an umbrella term used with reference to a group of developmental disabilities caused by neurological differences. While the genetic make-up of a person is sometimes responsible for ASD, the interplay of multiple causes often gives rise to this condition. Developmental researchers all over the world are still baffled by the 'why' and 'how' of it.

Symptoms could develop as early as the first year of a child's life or they may show up later, even by age three, and last an entire lifetime. Observation of the child's behaviour and their developmental milestones is the only method of diagnosis as medical tests, such as blood tests, are unavailable for this disorder.

The word 'spectrum' in ASD is significant as the manifestation and severity of this condition differ from one individual to another. However, individuals on this spectrum may display behaviours that are different from other people, especially with regard to social interaction, learning ability and a keen interest in repetitive activities. While one person with ASD may be non-verbal, another may be more articulate. As these characteristics may exist in non-ASD individuals as well, it is often confusing and challenging, even for professionals.

In addition, individuals with ASD often suffer from anxiety, depression, Attention Deficit Disorder (ADD) or Attention Deficit Hyperactivity Disorder (ADHD). Adolescents with ASD often experience difficulty in making friends with peers and making sense of behavioural expectations at home or school.

While there is no cure for ASD, treatment consists of the management and reduction of symptoms. Applied Behavioural Analysis (ABA) based on behavioural therapies is considered an effective course of treatment. Interventions, such as speech, physical and occupational therapies, help some individuals to overcome the effects of ASD, allowing them to lead a near-normal life. For others, the effects may be more severe, resulting in hampered functioning at school and in adult life.

WHO estimates suggest that one per cent of the world's population is afflicted with autism. Boys are more commonly affected by autism, with the male-to-female ratio being 3:1. However, worldwide, an upward trend in percentages indicates a growth in awareness or detection. The numbers may also be rising due to causes linked to pollution and stress. The incidence of autism is pegged at one in sixty-eight children in a 2021 study undertaken by the *Indian Pediatric Journal*.

For more information go to:
- who.int
- autismsciencefoundation.org
- autism-india.org
- forumforautism.org
- indiaautismcenter.org
- cadrre.org

Acknowledgements

I'm deeply grateful to the wonderful accompaniers on this journey:

- All my students who were a tad different from the rest of the class, thanks to whom a composite picture of the protagonist emerged

- Sayoni Basu of Duckbill Books for her openness, insights and gentle suggestions that have enhanced the quality of this book

- Rishita Loitongbam for breathing life into the characters through her delightful illustration for the cover

- Shruti Shukla, a fellow writer, for offering the title of the book, as well as her overall observations

- Fatima Rashid, an experienced psychotherapist, for validating the subject matter of this book

- Armin Arethna, children's librarian, Berkeley Public Library, for her engagement with this project

- Sunita and Ramesh Jethani for pushing me to pursue writing

- Mamta maushi for her carbs, barbs and mischief

- Evalix and Obelix for offering their home as a refuge from all other distractions

- Mum-Dad, Rashid and Lourdes Fernandes for their continued blessings upon my work

- The judges of the Scholastic Asian Book Award 2023 for shortlisting *Living with Adi* among hundreds of entries

Zarin Virji, a creative writing graduate from the University of Sheffield, follows her passions of teaching and writing. For over three decades, she has played the roles of teacher, teacher trainer and head of school. From 1996 to 2006, she edited the journal *Classroom*, a safe space for all matters related to education. Her first novel for children, *Gopal's Gully*, won the Kalinga Literary Festival Book Award in 2022. Her poetry and short stories have been featured in publications such as *The Research Scholar*, *Route 57* and *The Best Asian Short Stories*, 2018.

Read more by Zarin Virji

It did feel strange to see her lying cold and silent and then being carried away . . . But at the back of my mind was this growing anticipation—Sanjiv Maama was taking me to Mumbai!

When Gopal's mother dies, his uncle brings him to Mumbai to get a job because he has few prospects as a Dalit boy in a UP village.

Gopal is cast into the unfamiliar world of Squatters Colony, where he has no family or friends. He gets his first job at the bicycle shop owned by the sage Chacha and rapidly makes friends with the strange and diverse people who live in the community-Chacha's friendly daughter-in-law, the neighbourhood thug Raja, the three-legged Tiger and beautiful Ayesha.

And he learns that when disaster strikes and lives fall apart, he too has a family in the gully.

Zarin Virji's gripping debut describes the raw rollicking life of Mumbai's small neighbourhoods with vigour and zest.

Scan QR code to access the
Penguin Random House India website